ALEIKHEM SHULEM, GOM ZU OF GALITZIA

ALEIKHEM SHULEM, GOM ZU OF GALITZIA

MY FRIEND, YUSHKA GONIF

ED MILLER

To order additional copies of this book, contact:
Xlibris
1-888-795-4274
www.Xlibris.com
Orders@Xlibris.com
732672

CONTENTS

Dedicated to a world too easily forgotten,
a life too difficult to comprehend, a people
eradicated by modernity and the Holocaust.

PREFACE

The cover design of the author with Sholem Aleikhem in the Wall Street station of the IRT, in New York City, is an obvious example of *Narishkeit* - "Foolishness." Well not exactly. For in my imagination, it was he who inspired me to write these stories depicting the humor that sustained the Jewish people through 2000 years of Diaspora tragedy. It is therefore in that tradition that this collection of short stores has been written. Let us not allow that world of long ago to be lost, ever.

- E.M.

ACKNOWLEDGEMENT

A loving father, Saul Miller, tailor/author, who instilled a strong and enduring love of reading and writing about real and imaginary characters. His teaching all his children an understanding of Judaism and Yiddishkeit, and the rich culture in it. A family who helped and encouraged the development of witty, creative stories. Friends and associates at the Queens UFT Creative Writing Class who edited and encouraged the development of imagery that is so necessary to a story.

INTRODUCTION
Ed Miller

I was waiting for the uptown IRT train at the Wall Street station, on a hot August evening. The subway station was a sweat bath and empty, my having just missed the number two train to Grand Central. Impatient, I walked back and forth when a small man wearing a black gabardine coat and crushed velour hat suddenly appeared. In a broken English accent he asked, "You are Yu'ish?" It startled me to see a person wearing such clothing on such a sweltering evening and being asked such a question but I answered, "Uh! Huh!"

"Can we sit a bissel? (little) he continued. We ambled over to one of those wooden subway benches where he continued. "My name is Solomon Rabinowitz, but my other name is Sholem Aleikhem."

I should have recognized him immediately. My father loved him and his works. In fact, I began to tell him that his story, "Knurten" (Cnards) was Dad's favorite and had even read it to me in Yiddish, long ago. "But, wait a minute... didn't you die in 1916? My mother and father were at your amazing funeral. How come?

With his finger to his lips he whispered, "Shah! Not so loud!"

I laughed, "There's nobody here! I don't believe this!"

"Believe!" he answered. "I am here on a reason. You are my reason. No one knows that you are a writer and you have written a bunch of stories about the old country. How do you know about the shtetl (town) life?"

As I said, from my mother and father. "My father was a writer also, and he wrote about his own town in Galitzia called "Dobromil." Like you, he wrote it in Yiddish and it was translated into English for his grandchildren."

"So you know Yiddish?" Sholem Aleikhem asked.

"Well, not really! Like most first born Jewish-Americans, we lived in a Yiddish speaking household, like your own mishpukha (family). Papa even quoted you saying that your work should be translated so generations to come could read them. Am I right?"

"Gerekht!" (correct) with a big smile on his face, he continued. "I was sent to encourage you to publish it, but first, I vould like to see. You have in your briefcase?"

How on earth did he know that I had taken a copy to Xerox in my office, that day. I snapped open the lock and took out the manila envelope, drew the papers out and handed them to him. "Mr. Rabinowitz, 'Umshuldikt mir' (excuse me) but will you be able to read this?"

"Boychik!" (kid) he laughed, "You think I'm a greenhorn?" He took the first page and held it up to his face, smiling, "Yushka Gonif! Joshua Thief? Now that sounds interesting."

I sat there in amazement as he flipped through page after page like a speed reader. Once in a while he asked what a word meant. The occasional smile or nod of approval made me ask what it was that he noticed but he shook it off not wanting to be interrupted. Half way through, he said, "You captured a whole world of diversity in your "Plutka! From Yushka to Queen Leah! Shakespeare! Your "Dominoes" sounds familiar... mmm. Very interesting!"

I couldn't imagine why the subway train was not coming. It felt as though time was standing still. That no one else had entered the station also seemed very strange. In all this time, he had never removed his hat or coat, while I had taken off my jacket and was about to take my tie off as well when he says, "G'endikt!" (finished)

"Nu!!" (Well) "Mr. Rabinowitz?"

He shuffled the pages and set them back in the envelope and briefcase. "I like the way you fit foolishness into each story, and each episode in to just two pages. Where did you find so many characters? Some stories reminded me of my Tevye and Menachem Mendel (author). Yet they are original. I don't see a title page, have you any ideas?"

With a smile on my face, I said, "I think, maybe "Aleikhem Shulem!" Obviously 'Sholem Aleikhem' is already taken!"

"How about, 'FOOLISHNESS!' he replied, as the train pulled in and he disappeared.

All the way home, I sat there saying to myself. "I don't believe it! How can I tell anyone of this strange meeting. Surely, I would be called Meshugeh, declared insane. Yet, there he was, talking to me. I kept wondering, how did he know that I was working on this series of stories, and that they were based on the life of a poor man in a poor town deep in old world Europe before World War I. How did he know that half of the papers were there in my briefcase along with the work from my job?

Of course, it was the spirit of Sholem Aleikhem that had guided me. As I told him, it was through my father that I had developed a deep affection for him and his work as a child, and as an adult, having seen the play, "The World Of Sholem Aleikhem," produced by Morris Carnovsky and other victims of the McCarthy purge. The published collection of his short stories, had a profound affect on my psyche as did those of Mark Twain, Jack London.

Regretfully, I had not handed Mr. Robinowitz my ballpoint pen, that he might have made notations of his periodic remarks. Then again, if it was a spirit, but he was so real! The train pulled into the Grand Central terminal; and I rushed to make my connection.

I kept wondering, if the euphoria that I was feeling was visible. It felt as though my feet were not touching the ground, my head way above the clouds. I was transported to the world of foolishness that Sholem Aleikhem had seen in my stories of Plutka, stories that began with a weird experience regarding a weird town, where the people solved problems in a just, but weird way. If the beloved Sholem Aleikhem had the chance to read about Yushka Gonif, why not you?

Who else should be the story teller than an itinerant book seller, a peddler of wit and wisdom from the written page, for are we not the "People of the Book? Of all places, irony is the basic factor in their lives and survival. So, what has this got to do with Yushka Gonif?

Yushka Gonif

Before I begin my story, let me explain... In the Old Country, Hebrew names were generally "Yiddishized", so Yehoshuah became, "Yushka" and an appendage was usually added to denote some identifying trait, family, business or appearance. Therefor the name, "Yushka Gonif," Joshua thief. My story is being translated to English from the Yiddish for your benefit. I must apologize that something gets lost in the translation. As to their truth, I'll let you be the judge!

Plutka, is the name of the town and I know that this story is really true. I am a merchant, actually, a book seller, who goes around from shtetl to shtetl selling books like our revered, "Mendele Mokher S'forim", the founder of Yiddish literature. What was different about Plutka? It looked like every other shtetl. Everyone knew everyone else's business, personal and otherwise, what one did to eke out a living and so forth. Poverty was the greatest business, understandably. There was a poor shoemaker, a poor carpenter, a poor tailor, a poor wheelwright and certainly a poor Rabbi. Not unusual for a Jewish shtetl! So, what was different? Plutka also had a poor thief and his name was Yushka, Yushka Gonif. He had no skills or education, for a poor livelihood to make. He was so poor that he didn't even have a poor child.

Despite his condition of poverty, he refused to accept charity. All his neighbors took pity on him. Right after the Havdalah service, (ending the Sabbath) Saturday night, he would get to his trade and understand, he did not discriminate between the rich or the poor. As it is written, "Kol Yisroel", all the Jews awaited his theft and they all agreed to leave something around for him to take. From the frown on your brow, I can see your puzzlement.

"Crazy!" you may think. Not so crazy! That the townsfolk actually acted as accomplices to the theft, their own theft was unheard of. Of course it was unheard of. This was Plutka! A place unheard of, to begin with, and what happened there, surely unheard of! Well, about the theft! A ring, a Passover kiddush cup, an old gold coin. Nothing needed immediately. Nothing life threatening. In this way, the whole town provided something for him to steal. One thing Yushka did have. He had an excellent memory. He knew exactly from where each item was taken. This was important, so that no one else would be able to buy back the stolen item except the rightful owner. The opportunity for this purchase came on Thursday, when the market was held in the town square. There in the square, Yushka had a stand where he would sell the stolen items back to its owner for a groshen (penny) or two, depending on the generosity of the purchaser. And every Friday, Yushka would give a tithe to charity. He never stole T'fillin (Phylacteries) or a Tallis (Prayer shawl), items needed in daily worship. And if a person who was robbed couldn't pay anything, he would return the item, gratis. This is how he did business every week and this is how the shtetl provided for him, with dignity. What kind of dignity does a thief have? The kind that would maintain a Jew. The Jews of Plutka, no matter how poor, would never let another Jew starve of hunger.

Everything went smoothly until a salesman came to town. He took a room at the inn for a day or two and deposited his merchandise in the room. No one from outside of Plutka was aware of the arrangement with Yushka Gonif and the stranger certainly did not. Suddenly, he found his room was emptied of his packages. All his merchandise was gone. No help from the innkeeper!

He ran into the street, shouting, "Gevalt! Gevalt! (Help!) I've been robbed! Gevalt!" No one offered to tell him the secret arrangement. Everyone assured him that in a few days at the Thursday market all would be well. Everyone remained calm except him, they knew the situation but they remained mute. Understandably, the man did not understand, so he went to the Jewish policeman. "Don't worry, friend!" the policeman advised him. "Just wait a few days and you will be happy." The stranger thought, "What a crazy place this is! What a crazy policeman this is! And a

Jewish policeman, no less. A policeman who doesn't even bother to catch a thief!"

The man decided to run to the Rabbi in the Bes Medrish, the learning room. He waited, out of respect, for the lesson to conclude, approached the Rabbi and in a quiet voice said, "Excuse me!" He proceeded to complain to the Rabbi. He reported the theft, the policeman's reply, and the people's refusal to help him. When he finished, the Rabbi sent his assistant to bring Yushka to the Rabbi's Court. And all the people followed Yushka into the room. For the holy Rabbi, there was a problem. How could he proceed without causing public embarrassment to a Jew, namely Yushka, which is forbidden in Jewish law. He began thus. "Yushka, we understand your enterprise, however, to take advantage of a Jewish stranger, a Ger, does not befit an upright Jew. Why did you do this to a Jewish stranger?" After a pause, "Answer me!" Without spelling out the offense, everyone understood. The stranger expected a denial.

Yushka lowered his head in humility and began in a subdued voice. He said, "For a Mitzvah!" (A righteous deed!) The whole gathering echoed the words, "A Mitzvah?" but with a question mark. With this the rabbi became a little impatient. "And where is it written that it is a mitzvah to unburden a stranger in this manner?" Meekly, Yushka tried to explain. "Just last shabbas we read in the Holy Torah the portion 'Ki Sovoh' where we read that we must treat the stranger that is in our midst, just as we would the Levi, like our very own. For we were strangers in a foreign land. So, I honored this man as it says in the Torah, as one of our own. Isn't that a Mitzvah?"

The Rabbi sat pondering the answer. The stranger did not understand this logic at all. That in a shtetl like this, they make a thief into a Gaon! (rabbinical scholar) Make a sin, into a mitzvah! Meanwhile, Yushka's wife had brought the packages. She returned the merchandise to the man, who grabbed it without offering a word of thanks and fled. Truth is! I ran so fast, that I never heard the laughter in the Bes Medrish, in the town of Plutka, deep in the heart of the Ukraine.

The Flying Sukkah

Surely, by now, you have heard of the Shtetl, Plutka, in the Ukraine. And you must have heard of the Rebbes, miracle workers who were able to fly. But, believe me, this is a true story about a flying Succah. (ritual booth) Let me not get ahead of myself. My experience in Plutka should have warned me away but I am a trusting Jew, a merchant of books, with plenty of time to read as my wagon ambles along the dirt roads between one shtetl and another. So, I came to the realization that what happened to me in Plutka was not such an aberration, or fluke. After all, one finds such stories in our folk tales all the time. No reason for me to detour along my route to avoid that place. The truth is, I'm happy I stopped there, because I would never have learned about Yushka and his occupation. When I had the time to consider what had happened, it became less and less onerous. For the whole town to agree upon such a noble solution to a man's tragic life became very virtuous to me. In time, I too thought it a good story, something to share with my customers. I have to admit, I was wrong to flee as I did. You must excuse me, but again I digress.

This time, I arrived in Plutka just as all the men were busy building their sukkahs (booths), as this was the week following the Holy Day of Atonement. Ironically, I felt guilty for bringing poor Yushka to trial. I would have to compensate him for returning my things and to do so, I arranged for the planks needed to make a Sukkah to be delivered to his home. I use the word advisedly because the hovel in which he and his wife lived could hardly be called a home. The Mezuzzah on his doorpost was so worn by the weather that one could hardly make out the word, Shaddai. My deal was that the carpenter would not divulge who the donor of the planks or the pegs was. When Yushka found the material outside his door, he did not question its source. He merely said the "She'hakol" prayer and set to erecting the tabernacle. I had not planned to stay in Plutka for the holiday, having completed the little business that I could do there, when I received a message at the inn, inviting me to dine in his sukkah. As you know, it is a mitzvah to do so, but to be invited by Yushka, was a double mitzvah. I could not refuse.

I knew that to expect a feast was out of the question but the local merchants arranged to provide the necessities on credit, even though they did not expect Yushka to be able to make restitution. His wife did her best to prepare the holiday fare. The Challah (bread) was small, the one egg had to be divided between it and the Kug'l (potato pudding). The chicken miraculously made a soup, chopped liver, a roast and a feather pillow for the hard wooden chair. I left my own Shtreimel (fur hat) at the inn, so as not to shame Yushka with his hand-me-down scraggly one. Although he was a pauper, he carried himself with the dignity of King David. The fringes of his tallis (prayer shawl) mocked the fringes on his long coat. He received the holiday greeting with the same honor any member of the community deserved. It was a cool fall evening, the wind was apparent but not threatening. The sun had set in a blaze of glory, signaling that the stars would certainly be seen through the reeds covering the sukkah. Surely, he was blessed! He had a devoted wife, who had made a holiday feast, without a word of complaint. The tears she shed as she lit the Yom Tov (holiday) candles, set in potato halves, were for thanks, for the miracle that provided them with any holiday fare. In spite of the suffering, her barren home, the bare existence that her husband provided, she was treated with loving kindness by her husband and neighbors in Plutka. Who could ask for anything more? The candle light provided a warmth in that little room that I have seldom felt. Yushka and I entered and washed in preparation for the blessings. If Plutka was poor, it was rich in water. It was rich in piety! Occasionally, too rich, but that's another story.

The sanctification of the wine was made. A sip for each of us and the rest returned to the flask. Obviously, there was a need for frugality. The blessing over the Challah was offered to me, as guest and I carefully made the slices large enough for the mitzvah, yet small enough to satisfy the need to conserve. Yushka's wife brought out the food. I offered to help, but she refused my offer. As their guest, it would not have been right. We began to dine. I complimented every bite. I even sopped up the watery gravy with my slice of challah, smacking my lips with delight. We were so engrossed with the meal that we did not notice how much the wind had increased. There in the middle of the table was the pan with the potato kug'l (pudding).

All of a sudden, a gust of wind wrapped itself around the sukkah. Before we knew it, the whole thing was being raised from around us. We were not hurt in any way. It was a clean lift off and for some reason, the table remained sitting before us. Just the table! Everything on it flew away except the potato kug'l. We were in shock, for a minute, but we decided to retreat into the house. Our duty had been done. The question was, why had not the table flown away as well. The answer came as we attempted to remove the kug'l from the table. It was too heavy to lift. Only with the total effort of us all, was it brought into the kitchen. Yushka set about to say the prayer for our having been spared. The truth is, had the table been raised by the wind. we all would have been hurt. Yushka's wife prepared the kettle for tea and set about cutting pieces of the heroic kug'l. Despite the urging of the hosts, I feigned being too full for another bite. The hot tea was enough to finish off the dinner and we sang the Grace after meals! I complimented my host for his invitation and my hostess for the meal. I declined to take a piece of kug'l back to the inn. The wind had died down by then.

All the way back, I thought how lucky I was that nothing serious had happened. Who would believe a rock hard kug'l had saved our lives. The moon shown brightly lighting my way. Up ahead lay a mass of lumber, shattered but not beyond repair. Ivan, a local peasant was only too happy to carry it back to Yushka's home, to reassemble it, even add some anchoring. Yushka thought it was done from the goodness of his heart, for my compensation to the peasant was kept a secret. This was a town of secrets. How the Kug'l had saved us would be one. The only story Yushka told, was about his flying sukkah and how it was miraculously rebuilt the very next day.

The Dairyman

In one of the books that I've read, there is a proverb that says, "Every trouble has some good and every good has some trouble!" Well, my trouble in Plutka changed my life, not exactly for the better as far as wealth is concerned, but different as far as experience is concerned. For instance, I learned that the people of Plutka were poor. That in itself is no revelation but after several return visits, I began to learn about their poorness. Like all of God's creations, not all are exactly alike. There's poor, very poor and like Yushka, destitute. There's poor in wealth. There's poor in education and there's poor in Mazel, (luck). Even attitudes can enrich the poorest soul or make the wealthiest, a pauper in spirit. And would you believe, there's such a thing as half-poor. If there is half-poor there must also be half-rich!

Enough philosophy! As you know, I make my living buying and selling books, so obviously, I got to know who in Plutka could read and who could not. Literacy was not a necessity in the small shtetl. As long as one could recite the Sh'ma and the Kaddish for the dead, or unless one was rich or gifted, that sufficed. It is often said that Jews uphold learning as the greatest virtue. Well, not exactly! As I have found out making my rounds, there are many among us who are deficient in the skill of reading, especially outside of the Holy books. And so it was in Plutka. My sales were very meager there because spending time reading was not considered vital to one's existence. Understand, that in this day, reading after working hours was limited to the light of a candle or kerosene lamp, a luxury in itself, hardly available to the vast majority of Jews. And what could these people learn from my books that life hadn't already taught them. As I've been told, "Books are like diamonds, nice to own but not affordable!"

As in most small shtetls, Plutka had a dairyman. "Aha!" you say, "Just like Tevya, of Anatevka!" In one way, yes, in another, no! This dairy man's name was Reb Nachum and his wife was Sura Leah. Tevya had all daughters. Nachum had all sons. You would think that having sons would be a blessing. Actually, they were. By the grace of God, they were all brilliant, intelligent and all biblical scholars, who sat all day in the Yeshiva, learning, studying, debating. They were the pride of the Rabbi and the institution but did nothing to help their dear parents in Plutka. After all, it would be a sin to waste such intellect on menial labor, as was needed in the dairy business. So while their sons worked their brains out, Nachum and Sura worked! But that's not the story.

It's about half-poor! Nachum had a wife, Sura Leah, as I said, who was a good woman, a good helpmate. When their old cow stopped giving milk, Sura sent Nachum to the city to sell the old one and buy a new one and a beauty it was. Her fur was shiny, her eyes were clear, a perfect specimen and the price was very good. Everyone at the fair complimented him on the good deal he had made. The cow's udder was full of milk. That was obvious to everyone. He held the rope that he had tied around the horns so that he would not lose his prize. It was not until he got home that he found out what was wrong. Only two faucets worked. The other two looked fine, but something was wrong with the plumbing, preventing them from issuing milk. Whatever they tried did not work. Whoever sold it was long gone, so they were stuck with it. Half a cow! The great deal became the laughing stock of Plutka. Not to his face of course!

As it says in the Holy Book, "The Lord giveth, the Lord taketh away! Praised beith the Lord!" He and his wife were grateful that at least they had half. It could have been worse. Nachum and Sura determined to make do. No one in Plutka complained that since the new cow, their milk was half water, the hard cheese was half soft and the sour cream was only half sour. No matter how much or how hard Sura churned, the results were the same. They determined that whatever the going rate for whole milk, solid cheese or sour sour cream they would just have to charge half. On market day, they set up their stand as before. Only the merchandise was different.

So you think that was bad. No! For the poor people it was a blessing. Word spread to neighboring towns and the poor flooded the Thursday market. Sales were great. Unfortunately for Nachum and Sura the cow produced only half the milk needed to produce a full load of dairy products, so they sold out by noon and had to disappoint all those poor customers who came from afar. With all the success that they had, they still remained half poor. Then a renowned Rebbe came to Plutka. Nachum was advised to see him, for he was known for his great wisdom and holiness. At first he hesitated, for the shame of bringing his private problem to such a revered man. When his wife urged him to, he joined the line of those seeking guidance and help. He tried to tell his story as succinctly as possible. He thought the Rebbe would tell him to be grateful and thank God for what he did have. The Rebbe had covered his eyes with his hand, considering the plight of Nachum as seriously as he did all the others. Suddenly, he signaled that he had a solution. "When you milk the cow and it comes to an end, turn the cow around, facing the other direction and milk it again. It will think that you are using the other faucets and give you a full measure of milk." Was it nonsense or not? Well it was worth a try. The next day Nachum did exactly as he was told and behold, a miracle. The cow gave its full measure. Not only was the measure full but the milk was no longer watery.

Word spread of the Rebbe's genius and thousands flocked to get his advice and blessing. The Rebbe's coffers overflowed. But what about the dairy business? With the full measure of milk, the dairy products became richer, the cheese harder, the sour cream sourer and the price they had to charge, full. Instead of booming, business fell in half. The poor couldn't afford the luxury of full price dairy and other customers fled to other merchants. Their business reverted to its former rate. Nachum and Sura went on with their lives, accepting being half poor, just as God intended them to be and thankful at that. Truth is, I never left Plutka without a cheese from Nachum's dairy. A slice on a piece of black bread was a slice of Gan Eden (paradise).

Blind Beryl

Yushka was my guide through the history and folk tales of Plutka. Each visit was another opportunity to learn something new, something interesting. That the Klezmer (musicians) were coming to Plutka, triggered this one. I never met Beryl but his story was quite unusual. "What story of Plutka wasn't?" you may ask, with a smile. According to reports, Beryl was quite unusual. He was tall, handsome, bright and from the title, you can tell, blind. He was blind from birth. So! There were many Jewish babies born sightless. Most blamed it on the fact that his mother was ill and undernourished. Some blamed it on an evil eye. There were a few who claimed it had come from a curse. The consensus was that it was the will of God and that was that. The father left to make his fortune in Crackow and was never heard from again. Whatever she could earn weaving baskets from the reeds gleaned from the local pond, had to suffice. Soon after he was born, the good Lord took pity on her and took her to a better place, leaving little Beryl, a double orphan. The beautiful baby boy became a ward of the community, that's all he knew. He was a loving child and every family, no matter how poor, fought for him to share their humble home.

There were no bullies in Plutka to taunt him. None would dare to nor even want to. He was every little child's baby brother. He learned to walk before most children his age and his acute hearing and memory set him above the others in intelligence. In Plutka, no one could be jealous of him or begrudge him his gifts, for after all, he was the only blind person and the town orphan. No sooner had he learned to walk, than he was playing tag with the other children. "How was it possible?" you say. He could track the sound of his quarry faster than the sighted children could run. Besides, no one would knowingly put any obstacle in his way. The Talmud forbids that! Little Beryl never thought of himself as unusual. As far as he knew, everyone shared in his sightless world. Everyone in Plutka knew that the wrath of God would befall any miscreant that would harm him. Where ever he stayed, he was loved. He carried out any chores that were given him, cheerfully. He was grateful and joyful. He had an acute sense of hearing and a great memory. When the other children were struggling over the Aleph Bes, (alphabet) Beryl knew it backwards and forwards. When the other children were starting to learn simple sentences, Beryl was making up ditties like this:

> They say a bride is beautiful
> No matter how she looks,
> In my eyes she's beautiful
> By the way she cooks.

Moishe, the Melamed, (teacher) was so awed by the progress Beryl made that he spent time after school teaching the blind boy how to write the letters. You may ask, "What does a blind person need to write and how does a blind person see how to write?" Well, his teacher invented a system which enabled him to use the edges of the paper pad and a cardboard guide, so he was able to judge the position and height of the characters. "Amazing!" you say. I agree! Beryl was a wonder. The people of Plutka were amazed and lauded his every achievement but Beryl never lost his humility or appreciation. But that's not the story. Since he was very young, his voice was unique. Where it came from was debated. Some said it was God's gift, compensation for his sight. Others said it was a result from his hunger cries at his mother's breast for her poor supply of milk. It was said that his screaming made his lungs and vocal chords strong. If that was so, all of the Plutka babies should have been cantors. Whatever the reason for his singing voice, it was unanimously agreed that it sounded like angels and nightingales. Yushka interrupted himself again, anticipating my question. "How could he learn to sing if he couldn't see the words?"

That's exactly the beauty of the story. All Beryl had to do was hear the piece once and he could sing it perfectly from then on. At the melamed's suggestion, Beryl was to stay at the Cantor's house where he could study all the cantorial music and prayers. The Cantor was delighted to have such a pupil and the funds for the boy's upkeep. It was a delight for everyone concerned. Surely, Beryl was destined to become a great cantor and his ability to learn each and every nuance in the liturgy was phenomenal. Even before his Bar Mitzvah, he led the congregation in prayer. Word spread outside Plutka of his genius and offers arrived from matchmakers all over Europe. He was offered a seminary scholarship but he chose to stay in Plutka. Not one soul dared to refer to him as, Beryl the blind. He was called, "Beryl the Ba'al T'fillah! The master of prayer! The chanter." Since his performing of the ritual services, the attendance at the synagogue tripled, quadrupled. The child phenomenon made Plutka great.

As he grew, so did his voice. The soprano of his youth became the tenor of his manhood. His range was astounding for it stretched from baritone to the highest falsetto. He not only learned from the cantor but began to improvise and invent new expressions for the pious words. The Psalms of David took on a special beauty with his song. It was during the Passover holiday, that a troupe of Klezmer came to Plutka. From his room, he could hear the lilting clarinet, the crying fiddle and the rhythmic drum. As attractive as it was, it didn't distract him from his studies. One evening as he was working on his music for The Song Of Songs, he heard a voice outside his window. Surely it was the voice of an angel! As high as he sang a note, her voice went higher. Her trills were sweeter than his trills. As he sang a phrase, she would follow. When he paused, she paused. He began to chant his Song of Songs and she followed, word for word. His melodies became her melodies. As she was drawn to him, he was drawn to her. Their voices embraced as the words of Solomon did. The natural harmony of their voices caressed each other like a springtime breeze. He could not see how lovely she was, nor did it matter. She led him from the Cantor's house to the Klezmer's encampment. She led him into a different world, a different life. For this was the Lord's will. This was his destiny!

The Blacksmith

Yushka told me about Yank'l, der shmid. What town didn't have a Yank'l Blacksmith? He was a kind Jew who would give you the shirt off his back, which is funny, because he never wore a shirt. Actually, he did but not at work. He did not attend daily services because he had to get the furnace going before dawn and he had to "strike while the iron is hot," as the saying goes. He was kind and generous and charitable and why not? He was one of the few in Plutka who was gainfully employed. "Every Wednesday and Thursday," as the saying goes, he was busy repairing something that had broken and in Plutka, everything was either just repaired or just broken. But of course, that was not the story.

The inn at which I always stayed was very humble but hospitable. It had to be! It was the only one Plutka had. It had a small dining area for the traveler and a small bar to wash the dust from the throat. That did not mean that townsfolk were excluded. However, with so many poor, business from the locals was poor as well. He prepared kegs of home brew, a kind of ale, black as night, bitter as gall but it had a pure white foam and a kick like a mule. Well, actually, after the second mug the mule stopped kicking. How to promote business? He fashioned a banner and strung it up behind the bar. "Quaff all you want! Pay when you can!" The devil himself couldn't have thought up a better slogan. Most of the people were skeptical of such temptation and only drank moderately so as not to run up a big tab. Some of the wives did not allow their husbands the pleasure. Nevertheless, the inn was doing much better. "How?" you ask. "If the drinkers couldn't pay!" "I guess what he lost in credit, he made up in volume!" was Yushka's reply. I scratched my head, trying to figure out the logic of his last remark. If that was his answer, then I understood why Yushka Gonif was a pauper and not a businessman. But that's not the story, either.

The story was about Yank'l der Shmid. After a long hard day, he made his way to the Inn, the soot still on his clothes, the sweat still on his brow. He could have afforded a shnapps, even a brandy but he chose the home brew. The bitterness on his tongue acted as a balm. He was a giant of a man and when he fell asleep after six or seven, there was no room at his table. For most patrons, the brew made them docile but it had the opposite affect on Yank'l. It made him evil! He became dangerous. No one would even help him grope his way back home. His wife never found him in bed. No sooner did he get in the house, than he sprawled out on the floor where he fell. His poor wife was terrified! The first time that she tried to get him to bed, he lashed out at her, hurting her severely. She wisely kept her distance when he was drunk. "A Jew drunk!" Well, yes and no. He drank, it is true but a Shikker-alcoholic he was not! Before the break of dawn, he was up, washed, with fresh work clothes to start the day. The previous night gone and forgotten. Actually, that was not true. His wife couldn't forget, because he often did not just fall asleep on the floor. Too often, he would get into a rage and beat her. Believe me, he loved her.

Why he beat her was because of the drinking. Without the brew, he was the gentlest, kindest man. I think that was established earlier. For the longest time, she suffered in silence. Then one day, she went to the Rabbi with a question. He listened to her plea and sat thoughtfully for a long time. Then he spoke in a serious subdued tone. "I am truly saddened by this report. I know your husband. It is not he who is hurting you. It must be the evil inclination, Yetzer Harrah! And what allows this to take over, the brew. Let me talk to him." The Rabbi was about to put on his coat and go to the shop.

You would think that would have satisfied her? "No!" she screamed, "He'll kill me if he finds out I told you! You must find another way!" Her tears emphasized how frightened she was. When the Rabbi heard the word, "Kill!" his demeanor changed for there is no more urgent precept than to save a life. "Go home, my dear woman!" he said. "This problem deserves heavenly intervention. I will pray and ask for guidance." She offered him money but he refused. "A Rabbi may not accept pay for doing God's work!" he said. She thought to herself, "No wonder he's so poor!"

The Rabbi understood that this was an urgent matter. As soon as he had finished his prayer asking for guidance, he dressed in his Sabbath clothes and clutching the bible, made his way to the inn. The innkeeper was shocked to find the Rabbi entering his establishment. He waited for the Holy man to take a seat at a table, then approached. He took his table cloth and wiped the top carefully, for this was no ordinary visitor. "To what do we owe this honor?" he humbly asked the Rabbi. No reply. Then the Rabbi, curious to experience the cause of the problem asked for a small sample. The innkeeper left and returned with a mug of black, bitter ale with white foam on the top. The Rabbi paused to observe the libation. He grasped the ice cold mug and held it in both hands. He would not take a sip before he made the proper prayer. The innkeeper stood by and offered the obligatory, "Amen!" His own curiosity anchored him to the floor, waiting for the Rabbi to taste his masterpiece! A sip, then another. No reaction! The mug was soon emptied and the innkeeper replaced it with another. With every sip, the bitterness became sweeter. "Could this be the nectar King David enjoyed?" he thought.

"My dear innkeeper. You are a fine person and I would never think of harming you but it hash come to my attention that thish drink is making the blackshmith crazy!" He took another sip before continuing. "You musht take down that shign! You musht limit the drinksh that you sherve to Yank'l der Shmid before he kills hish wife! You wouldn't want that to happen, would you?" The innkeeper agreed to all the requests. Before the Rabbi staggered out of the inn, the banner was removed, cutting off credit. The innkeeper promised to limit Yank'l's drinks. I'm happy to say that the blacksmith never got dead drunk again. Never assaulted his wife again. Never fell asleep across the table, where the Rabbi could be found every weekday evening between Mincha and Ma'ariv prayer, with a mug of ale, black as night, bitter as gall, with a pure white foam on top.

Dominoes

Plutka was like many other Shtetls. I think I said that before. Our revered writer, Sholem Aleikhem wrote of his town and a story called, "Knurten." Actually, the way Yushka tells it, the story may have originated in Plutka. "Nonsense!" you say. Well, let's see. After the incident with the blacksmith and the ale, the innkeeper decided that he could increase patronage by making the dining room into a game room, after business hours. Games were popular in Anatevka, and all over Russia, why not here? So he sent for games from Kiev and set them up, one on each table. Several chess boards, several checker boards and one immense table for dominoes. Cards would come later but this story, I was told had to do with dominoes. Not just wooden dominoes, or stone dominoes but ivory dominoes. The best! Each game cost the player a fee to play that was the inn's take. Betting was a private matter. The Rabbi complained to the Congregation against gambling but the people who played claimed that they weren't gambling. It was a matter of skill, not chance. No one was forced to participate but the draw for poor people was irresistible. The pot never exceeded a ruble and it added to the excitement. What better way for them to pass the time of which there was plenty.

If you don't know what a domino is, let me explain. Each rectangular tile has a number of round dots, sometimes white on a black background, sometimes black on a white background. Most games have twenty-eight pieces per set. When more than two players sit, additional sets are added making more tiles available. Each set starts with a "blank" and goes up to double sixes. Look! I'll show you! In the big cities, domino games were a thriving business. Fortunes were won and lost over them. In Plutka, it was just recreation, not business. Well, not exactly. The inn made business. No one got in too deep, as to lose his house or property. After all, it was supposedly all for fun!

As the games continued, some players became more proficient. The number of tiles were counted mentally and strategies were developed to ensure victory. Soon there were serious contests arranged. There were large amounts riding on favorites and as the game proceeded, so did the excitement. So what was Yushka Gonif doing at the table? No he wasn't an observer, he was a player. But if he was a pauper, how could he afford to play? When he became known for his skill, he acquired several sponsors. Would you believe that he did so well, that he began thinking about retiring from his day job. Actually, he was becoming too busy at the inn, to pursue his career. The people of Plutka had a change of heart about their arrangement with him and balked at their being robbed. A tournament was being arranged and Yushka Gonif had become one of the top contenders. "How can that be?" you ask. Well, Yushka, as I said before, had developed an uncanny memory. If you recall, he had to remember from whom each item was stolen so he could sell it back to the rightful owner. Well, he also could remember exactly who made which move, which tile and how many were left in the pile. Few understood why he had mastered this game as well as he did. The inn became the center of social activity in Plutka. As the word spread so did the fame of Plutka's least favorite son, Yushka.

When Yushka entered the room, someone immediately got up to give him their seat. He no longer was dressed in tattered clothes but in hand me downs from the wealthy. His wife didn't ask questions. She just enjoyed the new status he was given. As the tournament progressed, more people from surrounding villages and towns joined the crowds at the inn. And I have to admit, I was among them. Yushka's cheering squad. I bet modestly at first but my confidence grew greater with each victory and so did my bets. Yushka did wonders for me. He did wonders for himself and the whole town of Plutka. Soon the final game was about to be played, Yushka versus Mushka. "Who is Mushka?" We're not exactly sure. A few weeks before, he showed up and got into the game. Mushka, is the Russian name for Moses, so who would question Moses? He was well dressed and had money. He took a room in the inn, ate well and drank well. The gold watch and chain were the real thing. Yushka should know. He was pleasant and quiet, made no unnecessary conversation for he too, obviously knew how to count. He rolled up his shirt sleeves before each game. He never removed his hat or the gold toothpick in his mouth.

The day it came down to Yushka and Mushka had everybody on edge. Just as the final game was to begin, Mushka pulled a long case from the floor in front of him. Everyone gasped. Was this a weapon? Was this a robbery to beat all robberies? Mushka opened the case and exposed a brand new ivory domino set. There were not twenty-eight or fifty-six identical pieces. Before anyone could say a word, he had dumped all one hundred and twelve pieces on to the table with such a crash that everyone jumped. "We will play with these!" he said. As Yushka helped turn over the pieces, he slyly examined each for secret markings. There were none. The tiles were clean, white ivory. The dots were red. Blood red. That was the only difference. Each player had mixed the pieces and taken the seven needed to play and fished for the extra piece to determine who makes the first move. Mushka drew an eight, four and four. Yushka drew a five and four, taking the first move. All around them, money was changing hands. Not groshen, (pennies) big paper money. The pot for the winner was immense. If Yushka would win, he would have become wealthy. As some players liked to do, Mushka held his dominoes in his hands against his chest, to prevent signals getting to his opponent. No one noticed Mushka suddenly developed a cough. Like a gentleman, he would cover his mouth with his hand, not to spread germs, of course.

The game was tense. Yushka couldn't understand that whatever play he made, his opponent beat him The numbers didn't add up. All the dominoes were on the table and the last move was made. Mushka had no more tiles, Yushka had three. He couldn't believe he had lost and neither could anyone else. The tiles were collected and the money, too. Mushka bought a round of ale for everybody and as they scrambled to get to the bar, he disappeared. Nothing was left but Yushka's defeat and the little red dots on the seat of his opponent's chair.

Hersh'l Hound

Of all the places that I loved to visit, was Plutka. Isn't it apparent? Sure, it cost me money! I never left but I gave a sum, not to charity, God forbid, but to help save a life. Anonymously, of course "So what has that to do with Hersh'l Hound?" (Harry Hound)) you ask. "Who was Hersh'l Hound? Why was he called Hersh'l Hound? Was he a seller of dogs? Did he catch dogs for the pound? Did he, heaven forbid look like a dog?" I feel so good that you are eager to hear my story. You noticed that I said, "My story!" and not Yushka's story.

It happened as I was hitching my horse to the usual post, outside of the tavern, I mean, Inn. There sat a scrawny little boy who held a more scrawny dog in his arms. The boy held out his frail little hand and begged for a groshe, not for himself but for his dog. I reached into my pocket and fetched a few coins, of what amount, I can't say, and gave it to him. Before I knew it, the child kissed my hand and said, "Hersh'l blesses you and I bless you!" I paused a little surprised and asked who Hersh'l was. He stood up and raised the dog for me to see, as if surprised that I didn't know Hersh'l, Hersh'l Hound. What I saw was no hound, just a bag of bones with long ears that hung to the ground like a Rebbe's Payos (earlocks) and a body whose rib bones looked like the black stripes on a well worn tallis. Sit, I cautioned the boy. There was room on the step for me, so I crouched down to join him. It was just midway between the lunch hour and afternoon prayer, so I made the time for the bag of bones and the boy.

I introduced myself and asked him his name. It was Mut'l der shneider's, the tailor's son. "And why isn't Mut'l in kheder (class) on such a brisk day?" Both he and Hersh'l looked up at me with soulful eyes and answered, "The teacher won't let me in with Hersh'l!" Actually, only Mut'l did. Hersh'l didn't have the strength to answer. There must have been a good reason, I assumed and with tears in his eyes, the child explained. "When Hersh'l falls asleep beside the wood stove, he snores. The rest of the class gets all giddy and the lesson stops. At first, the teacher had pity on him but disturbing the class was too much. It was either Hersh'l would be thrown out or both of us. What choice did I have? Besides, when I sit here, holding him in the sun, he feels good and every so often, I get a groshe or some scraps to feed him."

By now, Hersh'l's soulful eyes were closed in deep sleep and his snoring began. As weird a sound, I've never heard. With every snore, Mut'l drew him ever closer. He didn't hesitate telling me how he and the dog became friends. He was on an errand for his father. The spring thaw made the streets wet and muddy. All of a sudden, like out of hell, a wagon came crashing through the street, splashing everyone and everything as it sped by. "All of a sudden, something fell into the mud in front of me. It had been thrown from the wagon. It didn't move but I could tell it was a creation of God. My mom called every living thing, 'a creation of God!' I didn't bother to wipe the muddy mess from my clothes or the package that I was to deliver but thought only about the thing that came at me from the wagon.

"I bent down and picked up the dog. He was still alive. He looked up at me and licked at my face. I didn't even mind that my face was being slobbered on and my clothes were soaked and dirty. I found myself washing him at the water trough near my house. Mom wanted to know where I got the thing and Dad wanted to know where the things were that he sent me to deliver. I never heard what they were saying because I was too busy with Hersh'l." I asked about his name and Mut'l explained. The school kids named him. Hersh'l was very weak and he couldn't run. Mut'l had to stop and help him catch up to the bunch, sometimes he had to carry him. They would shout at him, "Hurry up! Hurry up! Hersh'l!" That's how he got his name. Hersh'l Hound! All summer in the warm weather, he gained a little weight and a little strength. In the heat he would find shade but when the chill hit the air, he would be taken to school by Mut'l and he would lie near the heat. "That is, until he learned to snore!" Mut'l sighed.

I got up and patted Mut'l on his head. As I said, "See ya!" I thought, "What a beautiful story!" A moment later, I doubted it. A moment later, I believed it. I disappeared into the Inn. As I shlepped my cases to my room, I kept thinking about Hersh'l Hound and Mut'l. I determined to be of some help. First, I gave the Innkeeper an extra few coins so he would leave scraps for Hersh'l. I went to the shoemaker's house and arranged for a knew harness for my horse. I had him make a leather muzzle from the scraps, to keep the dog from snoring. I made time to visit Yushka. I told him the story about Mut'l and his dog. Yushka explained that poor Jews in the shtetl frowned on having a dog. Only the rich had them to protect their property. What had the poor to protect? Cats were different. They didn't require feeding because they fed on the mice which were abundant. Yushka volunteered to check on the Innkeeper's supply of scraps. He also accepted the job of speaking to the teacher about being merciful to Mut'l and his dog. Although I didn't connect my donation of books to the school, to the teacher's acceptance of Hersh'l and Mut'l, I was happy it happened. Soon, I was on my way to other places, to sell my books and I was unable to get back to see my little friend Mut'l. Unfortunately, my route kept me from Plutka for many months. But I couldn't get it out of my mind. I just had to believe that Yushka, the innkeeper and the teacher all did the right thing.

When autumn came, I made a detour to Plutka. The Inn was booked solid and there were few options of where to stay. Yushka had done better, as I mentioned before, so when they invited me, I accepted their hospitality and was able to check out all the changes that had occurred since I was there last. When I had stopped at the Inn, I heard that Mut'l came by every day for the scraps. The innkeeper refused to take any money from me and promised to continue supplying the scraps for the dog. I met with the teacher and found that the muzzle had solved the snoring problem. And best of all, I visited the schneider's home and saw Mut'l and Hersh'l Hound. The dog looked well, and so did Mut'l. What a surprise it was to find five gorgeous puppies suckling beneath Hersh'l. Mut'l confessed that he had to reintroduce Hersh'l as "Hud'l (Hannah) Hound!"

The Coat

If it was an expensive coat, you would understand the fuss. If it was a fancy coat of many colors like Joseph's, you might be impressed. If it was a Shabbas gabardine, well, no question! But it was not even a coat. It was a jacket! A woolen jacket. To someone rich, a throw away but to a poor Jew, a treasure. Such a jacket one would wear in the spring or in the fall. Too heavy for summer, too light for winter, well, under a coat, perhaps. The place, of course was Plutka. The name of the owner will remain secret. "A secret? Why?" you ask. Because it disappeared! "How can it be returned to its owner, if it's a secret?" Yes, a secret and yet not a secret! Everyone in Plutka knew who it was but to spare him any embarrassment, as ordered in the Holy Talmud, it was kept a secret. How did everyone know? His wife went all over town asking about it, broadcasting its color, condition and the tragedy of its loss. The truth is that he was so embarrassed that he couldn't show his face at Minyan, he was so ashamed that he stayed at home. He couldn't remember if he left it somewhere or if it was stolen. "Who would steal a poor man's jacket?" you wonder. A poorer man, of course! And in Plutka, there were plenty of poorer men. It was a tradition that even among thieves, a necessary garment was sacred. Just as taking a man's religious articles was unheard of, so was his coat. In summer, that's different.

As you can understand, commerce in Plutka came to a standstill. Everyone became involved in looking for the jacket. But not only in Plutka. The outlying towns and cities soon heard of the missing jacket. Local newspapers ran articles offering rewards for the return of the jacket. As I said, it wasn't assumed lost, it was assumed stolen! Plutka's Jewish policeman began a search of all the homes to find the jacket thief. Every closet, every cupboard was investigated. If there was an attic, well, you understand. If it couldn't be found in Plutka, it must have been taken away to some other place.

The further away from Plutka, the more valuable it became. That it was an old threadbare piece of clothing was all but forgotten. Instead of a jacket with missing buttons, it was reported to have buttons of solid brass. The material changed from coarse wool into fine gabardine. Even the sleeves now had buttons. The plain jacket became a uniform and not just a soldier's jacket but an officer's jacket. Epaulets grew on the shoulders as did gold braid on the lapels. With every improvement, the value increased as did the reward. A committee was organized to collect money for the ransom because it was evident that such an expensive garment had to be stolen for the money. Not only was money raised in the Plutka congregation but in the surrounding synagogues and churches. On market day, every stranger was looked upon with suspicion and every officer with apprehension. Each neighbor looked askance at each other. Still the jacket was missing. No conversation lasted five minutes before the jacket problem arose.

The committee elected Yushka, formerly Yushka Gonif, to be in charge of the search In their logic, of course, who better to catch a thief than a thief. Excuse me, a reformed thief! He and only he could be trusted to solve the mystery.

Although every home had been searched, he decided to order everyone in Plutka to report to the Synagogue. Everyone, including the richest to the poorest. He called upon each to swear on the Torah as to his innocence. He had his wife collect the women and children to take an oath, also. No one assembled would confess. He traveled to all the towns and carried out the same routine, with the permission of the local officials, of course. There was a large amount of Rubles at stake and the prize was tempting. As time wore on, the excitement and the interest subsided. But Yushka's reputation was at stake. He wouldn't let it die. Well, maybe his reputation meant just a little less than the Ruble reward.

The daily life in Plutka began to return to its usual grind. Even 'anonymous' lost any hope of retrieving his long lost jacket. It was seldom thought of, except for Yushka's nagging resolve. He set about organizing plans to ensnare the thief. He designed scenarios and systems that would show how a devious person could take the item and hide it from an investigator. His obsession became so great that he began to neglect his enterprise leading to a failure in his business. The committee never met again and could care less. It may have seemed like years but in actuality, only months passed since the problem started. Yushka believed that sooner or later, the thief would appear wearing his ill gotten gain. Then he would catch him with the goods.

The summer months were brutally hot. Not only were jackets discarded but shirts as well. Fall brought some relief and soon the winds flew around Plutka and the leaves began to fall. Jackets were taken out of storage and were being aired for wearing. Even 'anonymous' had done well enough to have bought another second-hand jacket, pretty much like the one that was lost or stolen. He begged Yushka to forget the quest, but Yushka couldn't be swayed. After all, he still had a sworn duty to uphold. No one noticed that Yushka now wore a threadbare jacket, his business near ruin. He had lost his favored seat in the synagogue and when the High Holy days came, he could offer no large donation. How sad it was to see how the obsession over a simple jacket had wrought havoc with Yushka and his wife.

The winter months held Plutka in its harsh embrace. The deep snow imprisoned everyone but Yushka could not rest for the theft was eating away at his insides. He often lost his temper and his wife was frightened that he might be going mad. The Rabbi's appeals did no good. The congregation tried to persuade him to give up the search, to no avail. Soon, the days began to get longer. The spring thaw came slowly. The earthen roads turned to mud. The time for the special spring cleaning was approaching and the special preparations for Passover began. Every inch of the house had to be cleansed and searched for crumbs. 'Anonymous's wife shooed the cat from under their bed where she had bedded down for the winter. The long broom engaged the cat's bed and brought it out into the light. There was the long lost jacket! The cat had adopted it for its own bed. The jacket had been stolen and their own cat was the thief. ·

The Town Crier

Actually, there are two kinds of criers. In Plutka and the Shtetls throughout Europe, the Crier was called The "Shammas" (sextant). His main job was to deal with the needs of the synagogue, to bang on the podium, demanding silence during the prayers and the reading of the Holy Torah. Also, ministering to the needy. Sometimes the needy could be one like me. A traveler in need of a place to stay for the Sabbath. His other job was to call the men of majority, over thirteen years of age, Bar Mitzvah, to Minyan. Three times a day, he would leave his occupation or lack of occupation usually, and walk through the streets. Actually Plutka had many alleys but only one street and he would call or cry out, calling the Jews to morning, afternoon or evening prayer. Not that the congregation needed urging. There was little work to keep them from their religious duty. His job abated on the Sabbath, Holidays and the Holy Days, when there was no need to remind the Jews of their responsibility.

You would think that this job would pay well. Not enough for a crumb of bread! Money would have tainted the Mitzvah. Only one duty did the community have. The congregation felt obligated to keep his watch in good repair, Heaven forbid, he should err in the exact time the lighting of candles should be done or prayer should begin. But that's not the town crier I really want to tell you about. On one visit, Yushka excused himself to attend a funeral. Although it is a Mitzvah, a good deed, a duty to honor the deceased and console the family. Plutka was small and intimate enough to make any loss personal to everyone. Obviously, a Mitzvah is always welcome, so I went along. As I entered the chapel, I was struck by the screams and weeping that I heard. I thought to myself, "The dead person must have been very important. A beloved one, a noble one, perhaps a soul taken away in the tender years." The crying was so emotional, I asked Yushka who it was.

He shrugged his shoulders as if to say, "A nobody, a plain Jew! A no goodnick, a nothing!" This surprised me. With all that grieving, how could that be? In subdued tones, befitting a funeral, Yushka went on to explain who the person was in the plain pine box. In three, no four sentences, he summed up his whole life. The frown on my brow showed my disbelief. Still the screaming, the crying, the wrenching sobs kept coming from the front, near the coffin. Up front, not far from the wailing, stood the Rabbi. apparently engrossed in reading the Thillim, the Psalms. I began to ask something else when Yushka put his finger to his lips, signaling me to stop. The Rabbi rose and stood before the bier. The Black coat that he always wore seemed more somber than usual. He needed no signal to caution the assemblage. The little noise there was, subsided. He began with the traditional, "El Mawleh..." The screaming rent the air. I was so moved! Everyone was moved! He went on to extol the virtues of a righteous Jew, of the Glories of Heaven, of Paradise and the just reward of a virtuous, observant person. Of what such a Jew can expect as his reward in the world to come.

He quoted from King Solomon's tribute to an 'Eshes Kha'yil', "A Woman of Valor," to laud the woman who stood by the deceased in good times and bad, as though there were any good times. He talked about the widow and her long suffering life as a devoted wife and mother. "No husband could wish for more!" I turned toward Yushka and whispered, "Is it the wife or the husband that died?" Yushka merely shrugged his shoulders, confused as much as I was. The Rabbi lamented over the orphans left behind. Twelve! Eleven girls and one boy, the youngest. At least, I thought, he has a Kaddish. A boy who would say the mourner's prayer for him. He extolled each of the children in turn, how much pride the girls gave to their father. And to the son, barely nine, the heir to the fortune of debts. He pleaded for the children to honor his father's memory, to be righteous Jews.

At each and every remark, the screams and cries burst forth. It appeared that the family was inconsolable. You can imagine, when the Twenty-third Psalm was begun, everyone

in the chapel burst into tears. "The Lord is my shepherd..."
The song of David most revered, most read at funerals.
"Surely, I shall dwell in the house of the Lord, forever."
Nose blowing and coughing followed the prayer. The crying
continued, louder than before. I assumed a great eulogy
would follow. I looked at Yushka and he was dabbing at his
tears. Was he thinking of his own misfortune that God had
not even provided him with a Kaddish'l.

The Rabbi went on. He quoted the Holy Torah! He
quoted the Talmud! He harangued the congregants to be
good, to follow the 613 commandments. He exhorted the
women and the men, to walk in the ways of the Lord. He
shouted, "Here you see, God's truth!" He warned them not
to seek the wealth of gold but the wealth of learning, of
Torah. "Wealth does not follow us to the grave but learning
lives on forever!" he continued. I thought to myself, "Where
was the gold in Plutka? Where was the learning?".

I waited all this time for the kind words about the
man lying before us. Finally, the Rabbi lowered his eyes
to the coffin before him. In a solemn voice he said of the
deceased, "He was a Jew among Jews!" I expected more
but none came. Nothing else. Not even a name. The boy
rose and with the Rabbi recited the "Kaddish". "Yiskadal
V'Yiskaddash..." The bitter cries again filled the room. I'll
never forget seeing that child and hearing those cries. No

sooner than he finished that the pall bearers came forward and raised the box leading the family out to the street where the congregation followed for a distance, in tribute to the man. The coffin was laid upon the hearse-wagon and except for the family and the Rabbi few people escorted it to the cemetery. Everyone had to go about their business, what little there was in Plutka. The weight of the moment was heavy as we dragged ourselves back to Yushka's place. I swallowed all my questions.

I was told later, that there was no screaming or crying at the burial. Yenta was not there! Yushka took the time to explain. It was Yenta, who was the official town crier. It was she who cried at weddings, Bar-Mitzvahs and funerals. Cried! Even howled! For a price, of course.

Philip Friendly

It was only after my prodding that Yushka finally told me about Philip, actually, "Feyvil Friendly!" whom I got to know because he was rich. Rich enough to have a big house. Rich enough to buy books. Many books! When I used to mention the name to people in Plutka, the subject would be changed. Sometimes mention of his name would elicit an epithet, and not a very complimentary one at that. Why this person was held in such enmity seemed to bother me because my dealings with him were certainly favorable. Finally, Yushka decided to explain.

"Years ago, Philip was known to all, as "Feyvil Friendly!" As Yushka tells it, he was poor like almost everyone else even though he was an excellent tailor. When "Simon Shmear" decided to open a shop, he was the first to be employed. The conditions were terrible and the hours, worse. But his skill found favor in the eyes of the owner and he began to earn more than the average. This made his wife and family happy but not the other workers. Feyvil saw the inequity in pay and instead of keeping his mouth shut, he sought to get more for the other workers. His winning personality and great singing voice made the drudgery of the shop less burdensome but when he organized a work stoppage to demand improvements, the boss tried to fire him. Instead of the fine example of a good worker, Feyvil was branded a "trouble maker!"

It was hard for me to interrupt but the name, "Simon Shmear" kept nagging me. It needed an explanation. As though Yushka was placing a book mark to hold his place in the story, he paused to collect his thoughts. "The name says it all! How do you think he got a permit to set up a shop with so many workers? A shmear! How was he able to get such a supply of goods? A shmear! From the Mayor up to the Commissar of Trade. Each official, every policeman had a pocket to be filled. Shipments and profits were taxable but the heavy taxes were avoidable. "That's business," you say? Of course the payoffs were secret! They were illegal but secret. Don't you have to pay off the border guards to travel across all the invisible lines between cities and states? Simon bragged about it! Took pride in his ability to buy everyone! How else would he get the name? 'Shmear!' No one ever called it to his face. To his face, it was Mr. Simon!"

Getting back to Feyvil, Yushka explained that the shop was piece work. The more one produced, the more one earned. Fair is fair! The only problem, the pay scale was too low. Not only was Feyvil very skilled he was a master tailor. Mr. Simon offered him the position of foreman, to supervise the other tailors and he refused out of principle. Everyone liked him and respected him for his decision.

Then Simon Shmear offered him a salary he couldn't refuse. It would have given him and his family opportunities that were unforeseen before. At first, there were no apparent changes in him. He was helpful to the men. But when the pressure of business grew, his attitude seemed to change. He thought that their former friendship was being taken advantage of. He demanded greater effort for the same pay. His attitude changed. If the boss was tough, he was tougher. Mr. Simon increased his salary along with the increase of productivity. No matter how hard the tailors worked, their pay remained low. "Feyvil friendly" soon became known as "Feyvil find fault!" Nothing was good enough! The workers were forced to work way into the night. The outhouse was moved indoors to save time. Mr. Simon's quotas were constantly being increased as the market for his product kept soaring. More workers were brought into the tight space and more sewing machines with them. The more time went on, the meaner Feyvil became. He searched each worker to see if any needles or thread were being stolen. Mr. Simon was so pleased with the business, that he offered Feyvil a half-partnership. "What is a half-partnership?" you ask. Well, according to Mr. Simon, it's a partnership and yet not a partnership. It has to do with getting a share in the profits. An incentive! And so our "Friendly Feyvil" was now promoted to a half-boss. Surely he deserved it! He deserved a seat of honor on the east wall of the shul. He deserved a big house on the outskirts of town. He deserved a chauffeur driven coach for himself and his family. He even deserved changing his name to "Philip!" But he didn't deserve "Mr. Philip!" as he told everyone to call him.

The people of Plutka avoided him. He and his wife lost the friends who loved them not so long ago. In Shul, he set himself aside with his fancy clothes and Homburg hat. His wife's fur coat and feathered hat became a barrier between her and her former neighbors. Philip thought of himself as a rich man. The rich men thought of him as a servant. Just as the workers felt that he had abandoned them, the wealthy saw him as a worker upstart. His children were too good for the local schools and were sent off to Kiev from which they seldom returned. The greatest isolation was suffered by his wife. She was not accepted by the rich wives' clique and she felt uncomfortable in the shtetl. The maid she had did all the cleaning, shopping and cooking, while Philip was always away at work, so she was going crazy with loneliness. Without the struggle and the sharing, there was nothing.

One day, Mr. Simon broke the news. He was going to relocate to the big city. Plutka could no longer meet the demands of his enterprise. Besides, he was offered a deal that was impossible to refuse. The workers, although they had suffered, were devastated by the news. Philip was ecstatic!

A bigger place meant more workers, more production, more power, more money! And the big city had it all! He never expected that the news did not include him. Mr. Simon had no plans for him in the new scheme of things. The date was set and the shop would be vacated by then. Everyone would be out on the street. The workers had little saved but Philip had everything mortgaged to the bank. He would have to sell his home and default on his loans.

Then, the idea came to him. He called a meeting at his home of all the men who had worked under him. They agreed that they were all in trouble unless they came together as in the old days. They listened to the proposition and agreed to set up a cooperative with everyone owning an equal share. The empty shop opened as "Plutka Products" and began to thrive with happy workers and with a "Friendly Feyvil" among them.

On A White Horse

What a saying! How often I've heard it in my travels. The picture one gets is not what it means. For what Jew could ever be seen as a knight riding a white horse. So! What does it mean? It means that whenever it is used in respect to someone so endowed with glory, it has to be followed with three Pu! Pu!'s and three spits on the ground. If someone is blessed with a child that is destined for greatness, it would apply. If someone would gain great wealth or power, it would apply. Because Jews are prohibited from placing someone on a pedestal, they use it figuratively, "On A White Horse!" So, what does that mean in Plutka? Yushka tried to answer that question for me. Among all the hard luck stories, he explained this was the exception.

The child was given the name of Elijah at his circumcision. Actually, Elijah Samson, named for two beloved grandparents who did not live to see the happy event. This was the tradition among the East-European Jews. His parents were hard working and devoutly religious. Little Elijah was a beautiful baby, attentive to everything around him. His father worked at home and spent every available moment starting the child's learning experience early. Little Elijah, true to his namesake was a miracle. His memory was exceptional. Before he could recite the

Aleph-Bes,(alphabet)he was saying the bedtime prayers, the "Sh'ma!" This gave his parents great joy and they prayed for his divine protection. Everyone agreed he would grow into a fine young man but no one really realized how fine. His parents tried to protect him from the evil eye, because he was constantly praised as the most beautiful, the most alert and the most happy baby boy. As soon as he was able, he was admitted to the children's kheder, primary school. What happened was simply amazing. The child took to learning like a duck takes to water. His ascent in school was phenomenal. Each teacher saw the genius in him. Each teacher soon passed him on to higher learning, surpassing even the greatest expectations. Soon, he was invited by the Rosh-Yeshiva (principal) to come to Kiev. He was given a full scholarship and gained an honored status among the learned students there. He was expected to succeed and he did.

His mother and father were happy to know that their son was succeeding and heading to a position envied by most parents. His name became known all around the world of Jewish learning. As young as he was, his opinion on Jewish law was sought throughout the pale. Just the name, Elijah of Kiev, was enough to settle any argument of Mishna and Talmud. He was sought by the highest leaders in the Rabbinate. Offers came from the most revered Rebbes to have him join their table. When he reached marital age, one would think there would be hordes of women offered to marry him but there were none. He was too holy, too consecrated to his study to be involved in marriage. His parents rarely got to visit with him but they were satisfied that this was God's will. He was no longer the son of Plutka. He was Kiev's shining light.

The little blonde child was now a handsome young adult who was tied to his holy texts. His body had become frail and the hardy child now looked wan and pale. The Rebbe of Kiev saw the danger. He held a conference with the Rosh-Yeshiva (principal) and Elijah was spirited away to the Black Sea resort. Studying was not ended but a regimen of exercise and diet was instituted returning Elijah to health and he became a strong and vibrant man, a changed man!

Before returning to Kiev, he decided to stop off at his home in Plutka. The whole Shtetl came out to welcome him. He was the pride of Plutka! Never before had there been a son of Plutka to have become such a celebrity, a scholar, a future Rabbi among Rabbis.

Here I stopped Yushka. "A changed man?" I asked, "What do you mean? Changed! After a time in Odessa, by the shore, he should have changed. Wasn't he sent there to recuperate?"

"He looked different!" Yushka explained. "We saw the difference immediately!" He looked healthy and strong. He no longer looked like a "Yeshiva Bukher (scholar)." His long golden earlocks and beard were gone. Instead of the meek Rabbinic scholar, he stood before them, a heroic figure, a Samson. In fact he declared that he wanted to be called Samson instead of Elijah. (Later we realized it was to avoid the Czar's military police.) Many of the girls fell in love with him and blatantly flirted with him. That Sabbath, he was given honors accorded to nobility. It was a time the town would record in its annals. Little did the people realize that the change wasn't only physical. Something had happened in Odessa! When it came time for him to return, his plans were changed. He returned, not to Kiev. but to Odessa. He returned to study but not the Torah.

It seems that while in Odessa, while bathing in the health restoring waters, warming his bones on the sand, he saw a vision. She had a bronzed body like Bathsheba, with a smile that eclipsed the sun. She had laughed at him for his modesty. She had seduced him from his shyness. She had aroused his curiosity and temptation. She had arranged to meet him without his companion and to converse with him as no woman did before. She exposed him to a different religion, one without a diety, without worship. His secluded world made him vulnerable to the wiles and intelligence she possessed. He was mesmerized by her wit and charm. Though he knew this must be the work of the devil, he had no power to resist. She brought him to the tree and he ate of the fruit. The book she shared with him wasn't written by Moses but by Marx. He learned that the world to come wasn't after death but in the life of a workers' paradise.

His shorn locks had not made him a weak shadow of a man, it made him strong. As strong a proponent of social justice as any at that time. He soon rose in the ranks of the movement and became a stalwart against the poverty and subjugation of his people. He was becoming the heroic figure, that his middle name implied. He and his lady traveled all over Russia, drawing great crowds. His knowledge of Talmud gave him skills of argument, of dissertation, that few could match. So the prophesy in infancy, that he would become 'a man on white horse' came true, after all. Not as a Rabbi of Torah, as expected but a rabbi of Socialism.

Of course, we in Plutka were disappointed. Our image of Elijah Samson was very different from what had happened. That image of a great Rabbi on a white horse did not include a Delilah!

Shem Shlemazl

Somewhere it is written that a town is not a town if it doesn't have a Shlemazl. By now, everyone knows what an unfortunate person a Shlemazl (unlucky) is. Plutka had one. Some towns or cities have more than one but Plutka was a shtetl, so one was just right. Shem cornered the market. To all appearances, he was a grown man but in reality he was blessed from the day he was born with an overbearing cloud called, "misfortune". Yushka warned me not to get too close to Shem because "Trouble" was his middle name. He cited many instances where Shem nearly ruined the town. Just last Chanukah, he accidentally tipped over the Menorah (candelabra) and set the synagogue on fire. Some people had wanted him banned but they were overruled. It was not until I actually met Shem, that I too became a believer.

Shem was a paintner by trade. As you guessed, the yiddishized word for painter is paintner. What qualified him for that trade? After all the other kinds of work were eliminated for the danger that could befall him, painting was left. Surely, there was the possibility that a bucket of whitewash might fall on him but that would not be a critical disaster like a blacksmith accidentally burning down the town or a tailor, leaving a needle or pin in a garment to stab the wearer. Need I go on?

Very little painting was required in Plutka. The work was, obviously seasonal. The rainy season was out! The freezing winter with heavy snows, was out! The sweltering hot summer was out, so the only season Shem had left was Spring, and not just spring but the weeks before Passover. There was no problem of mixing colors because all the homes were the same. The whitewash (Kalkh) was simple to make. One part lime and eight parts water but for Shem this too was a problem. One time, Yushka explained, the paint was too thick. When Shem began to paint a house, the paint became glue and he and the brush had to be chiseled off the wall.

Of all the grown men in the town of Plutka, Shem was the only man with a cut beard. And "Why?" you may ask. After a day of painting, some hardened lime was too difficult to wash and scrape from his beard, so he would have to snip the hairs that couldn't be cleaned. Everyone saw that his fingernails were whitened but that was nothing special, for weren't the blacksmith's hands black from his work and the tailors' hands cut from needles?

It was a rule that no one in Plutka would laugh at a man's misfortune. Snicker, perhaps but not laugh, and certainly not to his face. Fortunately, he had an assistant. Well, maybe "fortunately" is not the right word. If there is such a thing as a match, they were a match. A comedy team would be more accurate. If one didn't have a mishap, the other would. That any house would get successfully done without some catastrophe would be considered a miracle. An example?

As is common in the small shtetls around the Ukraine, the houses of the Jews were four walls and a roof. On the outside, they were plain, on the inside more plain The white walls could hardly be called white, due to the soot from the chimneys. A blessing? If not for the gray color of the walls, the houses would have been completely lost in a blizzard. But, when the Spring came, it didn't look good for the neighbors not to clean up for the holiday.

These homes were hardly higher than a standing man, so Shem had little trouble reaching the top of the walls. Experience cautioned him against using a box or a stool to reach the high places. Why look for misfortune? Truth is, he would say a special prayer before beginning to work and most of the time it helped. He had many jobs each year but there was one job that had to be done, without fail. That job needed special attention because it was different.

Of all the buildings in Plutka, the only one that was two stories high was, you guessed it, the Shul. "Why was the synagogue with two floors?" you may ask. Because the women were ordained to sit closer to God than the men, so their prayers would have less distance to travel to reach the Holy One, Blessed be He. Anyhow, when the congregation collected enough to pay for the whitewash, Shem was hired for the job. Actually, hired is not the right word because he never took a penny for the work. After all it was a Mitzvah to do such a deed. Every year, he would take special steps to prepare for the work. He would get the block and tackle ready, check the ropes so they would not snag, clean the hooks for the scaffold and prepare enough whitewash for the day's work. He would even hire an extra helper, at his own expense. Having two on the scaffold made for better balance and faster completion time.

The townsfolk would stand around and wait for some mishap to befall Shem. Every day they would leave disappointed when nothing untoward happened. Once, someone called up to him that he missed a spot but Shem had learned that lesson, before. At that time he had reached over to reach the spot and caused the scaffold to tilt, losing his bucket and all. By now, he had become sensitive to his proneness to catastrophe, much to the chagrin of the ne'er-do-wells.

One year, not too long ago, the unforeseen happened. It was an early spring and the balmy breezes made Shem worry about his scaffold which might be caused to sway. He devised a heavy weight for ballast and when he tried it out, was satisfied with the result. Everyone was skeptical about his effort because the additional weight was seen as a strain on the ropes. Shem climbed the ladder, and his assistant did the same. The buckets of lime were hoisted up and nothing happened. All day, bets were taken and lost for nothing bad happened. The sun set. Shem finished for the day and the ladder was taken down and laid on the ground. He washed and snipped his beard and joined the others for evening prayer inside.

The next morning, right after morning prayer, Shem was ready to get to work. He set the ladder against the scaffold but was unable to climb it. Every time he tried, his foot would slip off the first rung. His frustration mounted as his effort was rebuffed. The assistant tried with the same result. At the Rabbi's suggestion, the ladder was taken down and put up again, reversed. It worked! Shem and his helper mounted it without a problem, now that the ladder was right side up!

The Sign

I pulled my wagon up to the hitching post in front of Yushka's home. "Thanks to God!" he had recovered from the economic catastrophe resulting from the lost jacket. I entered the house to greetings and hugs as usual but Yushka sensed that something was wrong. And he was right! It did not take much for him to find out why I was so depressed. What is funny, is that it is Yushka who usually has the story to tell. This time it was I.

The town where it happened was Brodna, not far from Plutka, a town through which I passed several times a year. Unknown to me the town was having a religious celebration in honor of their Saint Ivanov. At the entrance to the town, a sign was posted announcing that during the time of the Festival, the town square was off limits to Jews. This was not uncommon in this region of Christian Russia and especially in the anti-semitic parts of the Ukraine. The warning was never taken lightly and the Jews avoided the area for fear of precipitating a pogrom.

That a sign of warning was posted, I later found out, was true. That I had not seen it because it was obstructed by a large wagon, was also true. But neither truth prevented me from entering the forbidden town and getting into trouble. The local policeman was waiting for just such a violation.

He stopped me. He removed me from my seat and began to search the wagon. He spoke very politely as he escorted me to the local prison. From my conversation, he saw that I was an educated man but his duty was clear. He was a tall blonde man and he kept asking me why I had disobeyed the sign that had explicitly ordered me to stay out of town. I said that had I seen the sign, I would have certainly obeyed it. He agreed that it was possibly hidden but he had to arrest me never-the-less. It was his duty!

Because it was a religious holiday, the court was closed. I would have to wait two days for the Magistrate. That meant two days in the prison. I was afraid that my horse would not be fed but the policeman assured me he would look after him. As for myself, it was a different matter. Being observant, I would have to live on black bread and water. I had to fast.

It was a long two days, then my cell was opened and I was escorted before the judge. He read the charge, then asked the policeman to state the charges. A much shorter officer, with a heavy black mustache came forward. It was not the man who had arrested me. This one described my wagon and the merchandise I carried. He went on to state that I had blatantly disregarded the sign and proceeded into the town against the orders of the sign. I was afraid to mention that this was not the man who stopped me.

I tried to make my case, explaining that I could not have seen the sign because it was blocked by a large wagon. The other policeman might have supported my statement but he was not there. I thought my argument had merit but the judge did not. As soon as I finished, he began writing and suddenly stopped, banging a stamp onto the page.

"Guilty!" The judge ruled. Two days in jail and fifty rubles fine. There was an additional tax of twenty-five rubles. I was sure that I was in big trouble. Then the judge said, that because I had already spent two days in the prison, all I had to do was pay the money. Fortunately, I was able to pay, otherwise I would have still been sitting in that cell. I left the court as fast as I could. I said nothing but I thought to myself, "My god knows I'm innocent! Their god knows I'm innocent! Why didn't the judge know that I'm innocent?" I collected my horse and was grateful that my wagon and books were not destroyed. After dinner, we talked some more about getting snagged in gentile laws. We agreed that at least, I hadn't interrupted the holy procession. That could have been far worse, even catastrophic. It occurred to us that the obstructing wagon could have been put there purposely. Could the police have set a trap? I was reminded of a great story that seemed to match my experience.

It had to do with a favored Rabbi in the Austro-Hungarian Empire. He was in his carriage on his way when, it was stopped by some nobleman. The Duke had been friendly enough and when the Rabbi was asked, "Where are you going?" he replied, "Only God knows!" The Duke did not care for the reply, considering it a dodge. He repeated the question. The Rabbi answered that he did not know. With this, the Rabbi was arrested for being insolent and taken to the Duke's castle and placed in the dungeon. After several days, the Duke had the Rabbi brought before the court. When he was asked the question once more, the Rabbi explained. "Your Grace. Before you stopped me, I thought I was on my way to an appointment in Vienna. After our short conversation, I was brought to this castle. I did not know that I would end up in a cell in your castle. Only the Lord knew! Don't you agree?" The Duke had to agree and released the Rabbi with apologies.

Yushka had to agree that what happened to me was pretty much like the Rabbi's story. He was happy that everything was returned and that the horse was taken care of. I told Yushka, that I tried to find the tall blonde policeman to thank him and reimburse him for looking after my horse. But he was no where to be found. Soon, it was time for bed and we all got ready to turn in. We said our nightly prayers, and I added the special prayer when one returns from danger. I couldn't fall asleep because I hadn't been able to thank the helpful policeman. When I was about to finally fall asleep, I pledged myself to return to that town to find him, to thank him for taking care of my horse, wagon and my books.

Morning came and I told my decision to Yushka. He cautioned me of the danger. He even told me that I must be crazy. We washed and made the morning prayers, had breakfast, fed my horse and harnessed him to my wagon. When I turned in the direction from which I had come, Yushka could be seen holding his head in disbelief. It did not take long to reach the town that had cost me so much the day before. The policeman was on the main street. When I pulled up, he recognized me and approached. I tried to thank him but he interrupted me. "Please sell me two books that I began to read while you were in prison." I did! But not for the seventy-five rubles!

A Sacrifice Fly

"This one you'll never believe!" Yushka began, his hearty laugh drawing me in. Well, as you know by now, there were many stories that one would hardly believe and about a fly, a Plutka fly! In this day and age, flies are nothing new or special, so I set down my after dinner tea glass and waited.

"As you know, the tradition on Yom Kippur Eve, the father takes a live chicken or rooster and twirls it several times over the head of each member of the family and says some prayers to expiate the person from his sins. When they slaughtered the bird, it was considered a sacrifice for their sins. Where this tradition comes from, who knows? Anyway, Yossele's family could afford no chicken or rooster and were ashamed to borrow one from a neighbor, so they decided to sacrifice his fly, his pet fly! But here I am getting ahead of myself as usual.

"Plutka was no stranger to flies. All kinds of flies! Sanitation, as you understand, was not a priority, so there were plenty to choose from. On the hottest summer day, the greatest activity was chasing, swatting and missing. Plutka's flies were very adept at escaping their final reward. If it was a pest, God created it and up until it became an absolute nuisance, it was protected from slaughter. Some children had pets! If they could afford it, a dog, a cat, a goat until it was fat enough for ritual slaughter. It seems that Yossele had befriended one particular fly and it became his pet. 'Crazy!' you may say, but true. At home he kept it in a jar, fed it bits of sugar and food. Food! How much food can a fly eat? Yossele even named his fly 'Satan!'. Yes! Satan.

"The boy got to train his pet. He was so skilled at it that upon command, the fly would do whatever Yossele ordered. The other children would tease the boy about his pet fly but when the teacher, whom the children found hateful would become even more hateful, Yossele would whisper to his fly and the fly would take off and harass the teacher. The fly buzzed his head, his eyes, his nose. When the teacher tried to speak Satan would fly into his mouth. Soon the teacher would run out of the schoolroom to the hysterical laughter of the children. Apparently, this was no ordinary fly. He and Yossele were pals. He was so good after a while that just at the nod of the head, he would do Yossele's bidding.

"How did I come to know about this phenomenon? I witnessed it in Shul, one Sabbath. It was a brutally hot day and the congregation was ready to fall asleep. No one was able to sleep that Friday night, it was so oppressive, so nodding off during the sermon was happening all over the synagogue. No one dared interrupt the Rabbi. The snoring was ignored by the Rabbi as he went on and on. Then it was

'Satan' to the rescue. If I didn't see it with my own eyes, I wouldn't have believed it. Yossele. bless his heart, gave the signal and off the fly flew. At first he buzzed around the Rabbi's head. The Rabbi didn't pay any attention. After all, flies are not unusual, even in shul on the Sabbath. Then 'Satan' became more bold. He buzzed the Rabbi's eyes. The Rabbi tried to shoo it away with his hand. The sermon went on. Next, 'Satan' went to the Rabbi's ear. Bzzzzz! First the right ear, then the left and back again. Whoever wasn't asleep was trying to keep from laughing out loud. The dance was hysterical! The more he tried swatting the faster 'Satan' flew. Finally, the Rabbi abruptly ended his sermon with the promise to continue it another day. The service continued and the congregation was relieved. 'Satan' returned to Yossele and all was well.

"Only a very few of Yossele's friends and others knew of this relationship, a boy and his pet fly. "Satan' really was a pet. There never was a lid to his jar. He was free to come and go as he pleased but he never left Yossele. There are many stories about their exploits, too many to mention here and now. Perhaps another time. But getting back to Yom Kippur eve.

"The Evening feast, what could be called a feast, was ready and the family was assembled to get the father's blessing. But something was missing! The sacrifice! The

'Kapurus Hind'l'. Then 'Satan' appeared. What happened next, no one can believe. The fly took off and flew around each of the family's head three times as the father said the special prayer. The last one was Yossele. He had never thought to ask his beloved pet to be the sacrifice. Everyone was shocked when at the end, 'Satan' lay down dead! Yossele screamed, "Satan!" over and over again, but the fly lay still. Poor little 'Satan' was scooped up and placed in a small box. There was no time for a ritual burial. That would have to wait until after the Holy Day was over.

"Every year at this time, Yossele's family have the ritual sacrifice, only now they are able to afford a rooster. They gather round as their father twirls the bird over their heads, saying the special prayer and every year, Yossele, even now as a grown man breaks down in terrible pain, weeping uncontrollably for 'Satan', his beloved pet fly, who gave himself for the Yom Kippur sacrifice. It is his day of mourning, his day of grief."

"What a moving story!" I finally said.

Yushka signaled that there was more. "Since that terrible night, Yossele hasn't been the same. He seems to have lost control because he walks around looking for his 'Satan'. Every season, when the flies are in abundance, there is Yossele, a grown man, chasing after the flies, calling out,

"Satan! Satan!" People have become afraid of him. Some say that he is possessed. Children chase after him and laugh at him. They taunt him with his very words. "Satan! Satan!" in their sing song way. He does not bother them or anyone else. He just runs around looking for his fly."

"Can anything be done to help him?" I asked.

"His father has taken him to see the best doctors, but they cannot break through to help Yossele. They tried the help of Rebbe's from all over Europe, nothing helps. Some say, it is God's punishment for playing with the devil. I don't know. It is such a tragedy! He is a handsome young man who might have been a great success in life. Perhaps some day, he will find another 'Satan' to replace his Sacrifice Fly."

The Bodkhan

"There is tradition and there is tradition!" That was Tevye's favorite expression. Our people have passed on some traditions the origins of which have long been forgotten. Some of them have disappeared over time as impractical in the Diaspora. In big cities wedding ceremonies follow a new pattern, corners are cut, still a semblance of the old remains. When Yushka said that Feyvil Friendly made a wedding for his daughter, I was happy for him and sad that I was not in town for the occasion. Thanks to Yushka, I got a pretty good idea of the festivities. It was Feyvil's only daughter. He and his wife were going to do it right. If it was a match made in heaven, it had to be better than the best that Plutka had ever seen.

"The engagement was announced in shul a full year before the wedding. The bride and groom had never met. How could they? He was in some Yeshiva in Kiev. 'Studying to be a Rabbi?', you may ask. Who knows? The first time we saw him, it was in the shul for the 'Auf Ruf', when he was called up to the reading of the Holy Torah. That he looked like a Bar Mitzvah boy was no surprise. He couldn't have been much older. The blossom of youth was still on his cheeks. We could not tell if he was humble or if he was shy. You know, the shul is not that big but when he recited the Blessings they were hardly audible.

"The whole town buzzed with excitement because everyone knew the bride. She had grown up in a loving atmosphere and Feyvil gave her everything she desired. It cannot be denied that she was in love with the boy. Well, maybe not the boy himself, but a picture, a Bar Mitzvah picture. Anyhow, the girl was all excited about the upcoming wedding, her gown, her trousseau, her future home, her life as a good Jewish wife. And speaking of her wedding gown, silks and lace! Pearls all the way from Japan to adorn the bodice. Feyvil's best tailors did a magnificent piece of work. That she was five foot ten was no problem, nor was her large frame, for as Solomon wrote, "A woman of valor, who can find!"

"And speaking of the groom, he was no Samson! He looked small under the Shtramel, fur trimmed hat that seemed too big for him That she would tower over him under the khuppah, (wedding canopy) would be of little consequence. For he was expected to become a renowned scholar, a 'big man' in Torah. That they would manage in the nuptial bed was what counted. After all, it was a match made in heaven! Or was it made in the business office of the groom's father. He and Feyvil had done business since the children were little. Feyvil's merchandise was sold in 'Saul's

Suits and Coats' stores all over the pale. The qual
and the prices were fair. The two men worked hand in g.
ever since Feyvil set up his own factory. They both relied on
each other for success and when each had their first child,
they made a pact to unite their families as they were united
in business."

"At least it wasn't an arrangement by matchmaker!"
I offered.

"Nowadays, that has fallen out of favor, except in
extreme cases. For instance… But let me not digress. The
wedding day was fast approaching and all the arrangements
were checked and double checked. The tavern/inn was
booked for the grooms family and guests.

"That I was asked to be a witness, to have my name
on the 'K'tubah', wedding contract, was an unexpected
honor. I even joked at the signing, saying, "Do you want
me to sign, 'Yushka Gonif?" Everyone had a good laugh.
Speaking of laughter, they had a 'Badkhan', a jester. He is
a sort of entertainer, who makes up ditties to sing before
the bride and the groom. A court jester, for on this day, the
bride and groom are considered royalty, King and Queen."

I said, "I would have loved to be there. I would have
enjoyed the Badkhan's performance."

"I thought you might, so I scribbled some of the verses on a paper. Let me see if I can make out the words." This is what he read:

The Badkhan's Chant

The day of the Simkha's here.
Everyone was looking for
A happy wedding party
But the parents are too poor.
The Makhetenistah* is too heavy,
The Mekhuten** is much too thin,
The guests are hungry and thirsty,
Waiting for the wedding to begin.
The Rabbi is short and rotund.
The Khazan is thin and tall,
The bride looks very happy,
The groom looks, not at all.

The Klezmorim play off key,
The mothers trip and fall,
The groom stands saying T'hillim,
The bride's veil covers all.
The Blessings, the wine, and chanting,
The K'tubah is read aloud. Alas
The Mazel Tovs are waiting,
The groom can't break the glass.
Cut the Khallah very thin,
Sip the sweet wine, sip it slowly,
Enjoy the wedding simkha***,
For this union's blessed and holy!

* Mother-in-law

*** party

** Father-in-law

I waited a while after he finished reading. He leaned over and handed me the paper but the scrawl was illegible to me.

The smile had already faded from my lips but not from my eyes.

He apologized, "It sounds better the way he sang it. I'm sorry!"

"On the contrary, I'm happy that you took the trouble to write it down. Perhaps you could write it over again, more clearly. I'd love to share it with my friends and family. Did you get the performer's name?"

"No! He was only introduced as, "The Badkhan!" (entertainer) During the party, he dressed as a clown and went around doing funny things. The Klezmer played dances and the men and women danced, separately, of course. Even the bride and groom danced separately. I don't know if it was the wine but as the evening progressed, the married couple began to look perfect together."

Queen Leah

Let it not be said, that I was just a book seller. Without bragging, I have to admit, I'm a book reader as well. What else could one do, traveling long distances from town to town, shtetl to shtetl. As my business grew, so did my merchandise. As you understand, I included books in Russian, in Polish and so on, because among the peasants, there were also a few readers, intellectuals, you might say. You might be surprised but Jews are not the only people of the book. Believe me, I've sold many books by Pushkin, Dostoyevsky, Count Tolstoy, even Shakespeare, in translation of course. Of course, my stock-in-trade was our beloved Yiddish authors, Mendele, Peretz and Rabinowitz, I mean Sholem Aleikhem. But that's not my story.

As you understand, our people are great adopters. Wherever we have been, in this wide world, we have gleaned the riches of our neighbors. That is to say, without violating the Holy laws. The delicious Shabbas lukshen, the egg noodles that swim in the deep yellow chicken broth, was adopted. How do I know? We call it "Lukshen!" That's how! And what does Lukshen mean? Not noodles, but Italians. Of course it is not a polite term for Italians but... Here in the Ukraine, Mother Russia has taught us to make delicious pastry, running with honey, even better than

Viennese shtrudel. And it goes without saying, our blintzes and pirogen, thanks to our neighbors in the Diaspora, have become a vital part of our menu.

So what has that got to do with books? Once we learned other languages beside our "Loshen Kodesh," our holy tongue, Hebrew, we began to read books from other cultures, other lands. Our enterprising Jewish brothers saw an opportunity to share this wealth of literature and began to translate it into yiddish. Not into books at first but in newspapers, magazines. So, it was not so strange for a conversation over a hot glass of tea to be about, Dickens, Mark Twain, even William Shakespeare. In Odessa, I once heard a big debate about the English writers. "Dickens was an anti-Semite!" and "Shakespeare was a Jew hater!" Up to that time, I had no interest in reading any of that stuff but hearing all that talk peaked my interest and at the next book fair, I picked up several copies, in yiddish, of course.

I hate to admit it but when I read about Fagan in Oliver twist, I thought of Yushka Gonif. Of course, Yushka did not expand his trade to others. But then Dickens wouldn't have a whole story for a book! As for Shylock, the merchant, I cried for him. He had no mazel. In the yiddish translation, I found a very sympathetic portrayal of the Jew being victimized no matter what he did. Wasn't I a victim in Brodna? Was what happened to me a mere coincidence or a case of anti-Semitism? Plain and simple! Well, reading those books made me appreciate that our life among the gentiles was not going to be that great, no matter what. Well, the exception! Baron Rothschild, of course.

Getting back to my story. To tell the truth this was just an introduction. On one of my trips to Plutka, to visit my friend Yushka Gonif... Sorry! Yushka merchant! I saw an advertisement about a troupe of actors going to perform in the town square. Beside a musical program, they were going to do a play called, "Queen Leah!" In small letters on the bottom, I read, "Based on a play by W. Shakesbeer." I began to laugh to myself. I had just finished reading the story "King Lear" and by coincidence, this performance was coming to Plutka. I extended my stay just to see the play. I bought tickets for Yushka and his wife and couldn't wait for the music to end and the performance to begin.

The star of the show was the mother, an "Alte Yiddene", an old Jewess, a widow who kept bemoaning her fate. She had three sons, "Y'soymim!" orphans. Her older sons were very sympathetic, eager to help her by taking over the dairy business. They said that they loved her and would take care of her in her old age. They promised to keep the dairy Kosher. They promised to observe the Sabbath. She would be able to rest her weary bones, her arthritic body. All she had to do is sign the paper. What else could a devoted mother do?

When the youngest son came home from the Yeshiva, Payos and all, the job was done. He did not care about business. His business was God and study. He was happy for his brothers and as long as his mother was looked after, that was good enough for him. His mother spurned his kiss good-by and he left to return to the Yeshiva. As luck would have it, under the sons' control the business thrived. Koshruth was neglected and deliveries had to be made on the Sabbath. The sons got married and their wives hated the mother. Soon, more children were on the way and there was no room for the Old Grandmother. She was shuttled from one home to the other. Both daughters-in-law complained, "Who does she think she is? Queen Leah!" The sons insisted on keeping the Queen but soon realized that she was too much of a burden and arranged for her to go to an old age home.

In the mean time, the Yeshiva Bukher (scholar) had become a renowned Rabbi and was respected all over Europe. He believed that his mother was being taken care of by his wealthy brothers. Besides, he was much too busy solving other people's problems to check on his mother. Queen Leah sat all alone in the old age home, suffering and bemoaning her terrible fate. All her children were too busy to visit her, not even before the High Holy Days. The poor old lady withered away and died. The rich brothers arranged for a fancy funeral. The younger son was notified and prepared a glorious eulogy. (By now everyone in the audience was crying.) With the whole family gathered around the coffin, the three sons intoned the Kaddish! And the curtain came down.

The applause was deafening as the principles took their bows. Yushka and his wife were so moved that they could not get up from their seats for some time. When I tried to tell him that this story was written by a Goy (gentile), he didn't believe me. Of course, I had to explain how everything was changed. He still didn't believe me. And why should he? Shakespeare wouldn't have believed me either.

More Plutka

As it happened, I developed a very bad cough. so the Doctor gave me some herbal medicine and ordered me to stay at home. You would think that for a wife and family whose father was always traveling, they would be happy to have me home. Well yes and no! Yes! that they knew that I was still alive and no, that I was a pain! How could such a nice person as myself be a pain? Well, for one thing, the cough insisted on keeping me up all night. In a house with many rooms, no problem! In a house with one room! Understand? The herb that the good Doctor had given me had to be boiled and inhaled. It was meant for me to inhale, not the whole family. If it was aromatic, pleasant, scented with roses, it would have been bearable but it was awful. Perhaps it was meant to drive away the illness, instead it drove away the family.

The children, who love me dearly, begged me to get rid of the potion. Actually, they would have just as well gotten rid of me, as well. And who could blame them. If the medication was supposed to make me gag and bring up the phlegm, it succeeded. But it also had the same affect on the family. On top of that, the doctor ordered that the windows be kept open. In warm weather that would have been a pleasure, but in midwinter? The children found refuge in the Yeshiva and my wife, poor dear, suffered along with me. A real "Eshes Khaiyil"! (A woman of valor!) Thank God it only lasted two weeks or I would have been disowned by my family. The truth is, she prepared fresh chicken soup for me every day. I'm not sure, if the soup cooking was for my cold or to overcome the awful smell of the medicine. As I said, two weeks and the sickness decided to plague someone else and left.

Everyday, I had to make that awful smelling potion to inhale and every day, my dear wife had to throw the water out into the yard. I'm not sure if it is my imagination but I think it kept the neighboring animals away from around the house. Anyway, I was feeling better and on my route to sell books. When I got to Plutka, Yushka and all the people were happy to see me, as I was happy to see them. Wintertime is a good time for books. Work is more sparse and time is more plentiful. Gossip is a sin and study is a Mitzvah, a good deed. In this day and age, reading the Yiddish writers was a rewarding enterprise. Speaking of enterprise, mine was doing quite well. Pu! Pu! There should be no evil eye! Not that I'm superstitious, you understand.

At the dinner table, Yushka asked me, "Did I ever tell you about my Uncle Avrum? My mother's cousin. Although he was a cousin, we still called him Uncle Avrum!" Before I could reply, he began. "You have no doubt read the book of Job!" Such a ridiculous question! What good Jew hasn't read Job? "Well, my uncle was Job! But let me not get ahead of myself."

Part of Yushka's family settled in Poland, actually Austria-Hungary, at that time. The life in their town, Dobromil was comfortable and Avrum's father, who was the town butcher was doing nicely. His devoted wife helped in the business and their family of three girls and two boys all lived happily in that idyllic valley. Suddenly, without warning, this picture of health, suddenly died, leaving the mother with five young orphans. Yushka paused to blow his nose, hiding the emotion that welled up in his eyes.

It was decided to emigrate to America, where many landsleit (countrymen) had gone and so the oldest son, Avrum and mother went to New York, in America. Avrum got a job and worked day and night to help his family. He learned plumbing and gave every penny he earned to his mother. With whatever she had been able to save, she bought a dairy business on the East Side. "I would never have known all this except for the letters that I received. Would you believe that I saved every one, in the attic." Anyhow, they soon had enough to send for the other children. The family grew up without a father. So many other things come to mind but let me not stray. Avrum found a beautiful bride and had a family of his own. He had become very prosperous and his wife enjoyed his good fortune, until hard times came. She left him and the children! No good-by! No "GET" (divorce), nothing. He tried to win her back but she refused. He pursued her until one day a "Shtarker" (hoodlum) threatened his life. He gave up! His sons had to fend for themselves.

He learned a new trade, 'Locksmith' and built himself a large cart in which to carry his tools and his wares. Funny, you should ask, "What about the rest of his family?" Like Job, they all had forsaken him. All except one sister, 'the Eidel one', who opened her home and her heart to him, no matter what. Avrum could not afford a horse to pull the heavy cart, so he would pull it by himself, from state to state, from town to town, to eke out a living. He was a middle aged man, strong enough to carry his load. Very often, he would pull up beside of the road to sleep, huddled against the cold and the rain. Never did he complain! Never did he curse God for his undeserved misery. Sometimes, one of the local Gentiles would let him sleep in their barn, out of the bitter cold, offer him a meal, out of Christian charity. If they found out that he was a Jew, they wouldn't believe it, because all the Jews were rich! They couldn't believe that one of God's chosen people would be pulling a heavy cart of keys up and down the hills of Pennsylvania.

One letter from his brother-in-law told how Avrum surprised them. It was the Passover Seder and just when the younger daughter opened the door for Eliyahu Hanavi (Elijah, the prophet) to come in, Avrum stepped in the door. He had arranged to leave his wares with a farmer, so he could hitch hike all the way, to be with the only home where he was welcome. He stayed a week, for only there could he observe the Passover kashruth. Yushka paused, taken with emotion.

Somewhere along the way, Avrum explained, he had found an old discarded fiddle. The case was broken and the strings were worn but he repaired it enough so that it would play. Avrum was left handed and had to restring the instrument to play it. With great patience, he struggled to give it life and it repaid him with sounds of music. He taught himself the finger positions. He taught himself the melodies. For this was the only reward that God had granted him on his long perilous journey. His sister sent him off with warm clothing, and enough money to travel back by bus. He promised upon his return, he would teach his young nephew how to play.

Moses and Aaron

Yushka assured me this was not about Moses and Aaron of the Bible, although, coincidentally, they also had a sister, Miriam. Miriam and her husband came to live in Plutka soon after the 1902 pogroms in the Ukraine. Their whole family was massacred and their house burned to the ground by the Cossack marauders and had they not as youngsters escaped into the woods, they too would have been among the victims. When they returned, they decided to leave that place after dutifully burying the dead. Miriam's husband had family in Plutka and so she decided to settle here while her brothers sought better opportunity in the seashore town of Odessa.

Miriam helped her husband set up a cobbler shop which soon succeeded well enough to become a thriving business. Women came from all over the area to buy his high grade fancy footwear which with the help of his wife Miriam developed a steady clientele. Soon they were blessed with a beautiful baby girl, whom they named for her dear mother lost in the pogrom. But that's not the story. The story takes place in Odessa.

The two brothers, although not close in age, decided to buy a house together. They both had wives by then and it made sense at the time to pool their resources. Everything seemed to go along well, or so it seemed. The men went to work in different industries which gave them little time to socialize or concern themselves with the affairs of the home. Not so the wives. Each woman came from a different background and although they both were observant, they had differences in life's perspective. The older brother's wife was set in her ways. She held to the old shtetl beliefs. Although her husband Moses was tolerant, he became interested in the modern philosophy of Socialism. He saw himself as a worker and as long as he made a decent living, he was satisfied. He became involved in the "Arbeiter Farband", the Jewish workers' organization. The other brother saw opportunity in enterprise. No sooner had he learned the skills of his trade than he bought into the business and began reaping a percentage of the profits.

The brothers decided to upgrade their location and soon found a house in a better neighborhood, still too expensive for each alone, so they went on to share the new home, one family above the other. That Aaron took the top floor was accepted, because his income was definitely better. For the brothers, that was no matter of consequence but for their wives, it was a different matter. The upper floor held greater prestige because it was more private. To get to the upper floor, one had to pass through the lower one. Aaron's wife found fault with everything Moses' wife did. Whatever her sister-in-law cooked sent objectionable odors up to the second floor. Whatever noise came from the top floor became intolerable to the family below. The only conversation between the two women, was complaints, some valid, most, nonsense.

Moses was blessed with two boys, Aaron with two girls. The children were told to keep away from their cousins. They could not understand why. To satisfy their mothers, they pretended to oblige but they met secretly, their love for each other too strong to be severed by their mothers. Little acts of spite increased the animus between the two women. Each woman reported her version of the other woman's evil to her spouse. At first, the brothers remained aloof but in time the argument became theirs. Each husband, unaware of the problem's genesis took the word of their own wife as truth. Neither brother took the time to rationally discuss the situation with the other. The venom increased and the brothers saw no end but separation. The only information that Miriam received was by mail and each letter from the brothers told two stories. Her pleas for reconciliation went unheeded.

Their separation needed settling the sale of the house. Each claimed the lion's share of the money and the animosity accelerated. Neither was satisfied with the court's decision. One thing they agreed upon, was never to see or speak to each other again. For the wives it was perfect. For the brothers it was unfortunate. For their sister Miriam, it was devastating. None of her pleas did any good. She decided to go to Odessa to talk to her brothers. Neither would be moved. They and their new homes would be off limits to the other brother and his family. Time passed and nothing changed except the hatred. Miriam's pain at seeing her family, that had survived the terror of the worst pogrom in history, die at the hands of hatred.

Miriam received an invitation to Moses's son's Bar Mitzvah. The boy was the family pride, a beautiful child, brilliant student, a scholar steeped in religion and Yiddishkeit. She ached to be with her family for such a momentous occasion. Of all the children, her older brother was the only one who could celebrate a family Bar-Mitzvah. She sent a letter to Moses. The reply came that Aaron had not been invited. She refused to come. All the pleading from Moses would not persuade her to change her mind. She could not attend, no matter how sorry she felt. If Aaron and his family were excluded, she would not go. And she did not. She could not, not without her other brother. She sent her husband to the party. And that was it!

Miriam's husband took Moses aside. He explained how badly Miriam had felt. He tried to explain how Miriam was being punished for something she was completely innocent of. He tried to put the whole foolishness into perspective. The fault was no-one's! It was an error of judgment. The good decision to share a house had gone sour. He followed with questions. "Do you love your sister? Do you love your children? Do you love your brother? Why do you keep punishing them and yourself? Does it make sense?" He did not need a reply. From the look of pain in Moses' eyes, the answer was clear. Then came the clincher. "Do you want to see your sister?" That was the only question that needed a reply. With his positive reply came the conditions. "Have a family reunion! Include Aaron and his family! There is to be no talking to each other. Miriam will come if Aaron agrees. The wives must sit apart, no talking, also." When he left Moses, he was satisfied with the agreement. Miriam's husband went to Aaron with the same questions and conditions. At the reunion, the parents sat along the walls, the children in the middle of the floor playing together, the way cousins do. The message was clear! The adults got the message, 'if only for the sake of the children!' And Miriam!

Invitation

It is always nice to receive an invitation to a Simkha, a happy occasion. Sometimes, when business prevents my attendance, I send my regrets with a generous gift. Sometimes the invitation comes as a matter of form, a sort of announcement where the attendance is really not anticipated, when no arrangements are offered for staying over, no accommodations planned, considering the distance, inconvenience and hardship of getting to the occasion. Actually, this kind of invitation could be as hurtful as not getting invited at all.

In the good old days, an announcement in Shul the week before meant that everyone was invited, including family, friends and the congregation. Yushka and I were enjoying a restful Sabbath afternoon, when this subject came up. Yushka was taking up the conversation.

"I remember one Bar Mitzvah, years ago. There were many out-of-town guests and the Shul was full. The women's gallery was also overflowing, not only with women but young girls, for the boy was very popular in Plutka. He was kind and considerate, always being courteous and helpful, seeking no reward. Although he was not very tall, he was very handsome, well groomed and had a golden voice. His parents were not wealthy but comfortable enough to make a nice celebration. They had arranged for the visitors to stay at the tavern/inn and the overflow as guests at private homes. I had the pleasure of having an Uncle and Aunt stay with us. A gracious and well educated man who has since become a friend by correspondence.

"Not every Bar Mitzvah is capable or educated enough to read the whole portion from the Holy Torah, besides the Haftorah and Blessings, but this boy did. The thought of his high sweet tones still bring tears to my eyes. What clarity of tone! Every word a pearl! As is our custom, the women throw down fruits, nuts and candy as soon as the last Haftorah blessing is sung. These symbols of good wishes did not rain down on him, it was a blizzard. The Shammas had to bang over and over again to remind us that this was not a concert but a shul.

"The Uncle of the Bar Mitzvah, a fine man with a beautiful baritone voice, rose to chant the Musaf, afternoon Sabbath prayer. What a surprise to see that it was our very own house guest. As fine an Ashkenzi rendering as I have ever heard. Had he lived close by, I would have offered him the Cantor's job. As is customary, a small Kiddush, wine and cake, is offered the regular congregation in the Tallis room, and a larger Kiddush in the Bes Medrish, study hall, with Challah, herring and gefilte fish, egg salad, Shnapps and wine for the guests of the Bar Mitzvah. The services ended and the Kiddush was announced, inviting the congregation and guests. The small Kiddush that was prepared was overlooked.

"A flock of vultures couldn't have done a better job of cleaning up every morsel of food. By the time the immediate family and guests had descended to the feast, there was none. They had not even waited for the Rabbi to make the Kiddush over the wine or the blessing over the Challah. Even they had gone! The Parents of the Bar Mitzvah were embarrassed, devastated. The rabbi calmed them and reminded them that all was not lost. He sent his Shammas up to the Tallis room to bring down the wine and Challah. The boy's father was offered to make the Sanctification prayer over the wine and the Uncle was honored with the blessing over the Challah. As to the family and guests, they were all invited to the Tavern for a luncheon as guests of the proprietor and his wife. It was a glorious day and one that everyone would always remember."

"That was generous of the Taverner!" I said. "He really saved the day!"

"Well, actually, it was mutual. The parents of the Bar Mitzvah not only arranged for guests to stay at the tavern but they had arranged for a celebration feast to be held that evening and a breakfast the next day. Besides a sumptuous meal that evening, the Bar Mitzvah gave a beautiful speech, thanking everyone for coming, for their gifts and their love. Not one word was said to remind us about the near catastrophe of that afternoon, nor was it necessary."

Suddenly, I noticed tears welling up in Yushka's eyes. A great sadness seemed to come over him. It couldn't be the Bar Mitzvah story. "Yushka!" I whispered, "What's wrong?"

"It's nothing!" he began. "Simchas just reminded me of Uncle Avrum. You remember what a tragic existence he had. Jewish families were very close, even extended families and Landsleit. From the letters that I received, there in the city, New York where the people lived on top of each other, they were even more close. But then some, who became better off moved away to a Brooklyn. Still, every chance they had they came together. Avrum's wife was America born and cared nothing for the family from Europe. When occasions came, he would take his son to attend. He always had some 'white lie' to excuse her absence. After she threw him out, and conditions were worse, he became reticent to get together with his people. Even his immediate family shunned him. All except for one sister and her husband, who would never desert him. As on the Passover incident, you recall, their door was always open to him as it was to everyone. The truth is that there was a standing invitation in their home, "All Welcome!" The youngest son, seeing a half empty shnapps bottle high up on a shelf, asked, 'Who is that for?' He was told, it's special for Uncle Avrum, when he comes, to warm his weary bones!"

I had to interject, "With all his miserable luck, he was a lucky man!"

"Well, that's not the story. As happens, in families, there are joyful times and sad times. Avrum's Great-Uncle passed away. He was a beloved man, a charitable man, a devout man, one who practiced the 613 Mitzvos as much as reciting them. Everyone loved this man and revered him. The assemblage at his funeral filled the shul, where his coffin was placed and the surrounding streets. It was a hard decision for Avrum not to attend but in his torn clothing, he felt ashamed. He stood outside the mourners' home hesitating before he entered, to express his condolence at the Shivah. He was greeted with a shriek from his widowed aunt "Now you come to me in my time of grief? Where were you in my joy? My simchas? Get out!" Her screams tore at every soul. Avrum could not explain that his poverty and shame had prevented it! He had come to every occasion, had looked in at the window, but left. Too embarrassed to attend."

Plutka Pickles

Why I woke up this morning with the name "Plutka Pickles" on my mind, I don't know. Maybe it was the tingling sour taste in my mouth or the invitation to a celebration that I received from Yushka, the day before. Plutka Pickles, if you haven't heard by now are the purest, tastiest, most aromatic, not to say most delicious product that the name Plutka can be associated with. Chaim was the last in a line of magicians to make pickles, a line that might go back as far as the bazaar days in our Holy city, Jerusalem, 2000 years ago. As you remember, trade in spices was not uncommon way back then and it is the spices that make the pickling.

Other cities and other towns have there own picklers, and as a traveling book seller, I can attest to their quality but none had the magic of Chaim's pickles. You may ask, "Magic?" Yes! Magic! Even before you sat down at the table, the spell began to work. The smell chased you wherever you were, inciting you to cheat, to steal a bite. Many family battles started with a mother forbidding a child from grabbing a pickle before the Sabbath dinner. Many fathers had to chastise a child who couldn't withstand the angel of temptation. And believe me, this was not only in Plutka because Chaim's pickles were sold all over the Ukraine, to Jews and Non-Jews alike.

As I mentioned, his family were picklers forever: cucumbers, tomatoes, sweet, hot, crunchy, soft. If there was a barrel, if there was a glass jar, Chaim's pickles were in it. Very often, as I traveled from town to town, the wagon would pass me with the picture of a happy pickle on its canvas cover. Business was good, even in the worst of times. "Worst of times?" Yushka once told me that the people of Plutka would hide in Chaim's basement during a pogrom because the Anti-Semitic Cossacks would never harm the pickle maker. The children of the very poor would go out of their way to and from school to inhale the smells that surrounded Chaim's home. Too poor to buy but not too poor to sniff.

"Didn't he have a shop?" No! His family had always kept the business in their house to protect the secret spices from being stolen. The secret recipe was so sacrosanct that only the oldest son was heir to it, according to Jewish inheritance law. I can just imagine, the special rite that took place right after the boy's Bar Mitzvah, when he would be sworn to secrecy, having been given the magic recipes. It was Chaim's third wife who decided to expand the stock to include other vegetables. She decided to pickle the beets left over after making the traditional Borsht, and carrots, sweet and sour. If it was an edible vegetable, she pickled it. Everything except meats and fish.

Those delicacies were left to the butcher and the dairyman. In good times and even not so good times, Chaim's business thrived. Only two times were there problems. When the weather destroyed the vegetable crops and when the depression destroyed the market for pickles. For years, I thought pickles can't spoil because of the spices and preservatives. Well, I found out that I was mistaken. Yushka laughed when I told him this and explained it to me.

"Under most weather conditions, pickles last a very long time but sitting in the barrel too long can be a problem. The sediment has to be discarded and the barrels washed thoroughly and purged before a new batch of vegetables can be pickled. I'm sure you didn't know that certain things have to be allowed different amounts of time to mature. Different vegetables require smaller size barrels and others, larger ones. Some things need cool and some normal temperatures, and that was the problem one summer.

"The weather was so hot and dry that there was a drought. The land dried up and so did the crops. Whatever food there was, was needed to be eaten, not pickled. All of this affected the market and Chaim's fancy pickles remained in the barrels. With the intense heat, the merchandise became rancid, the smell unbearable. His neighbors who used to love the aroma emanating from his house, began to complain. Not only could he not sell his pickles, they became a nuisance and had to be discarded. Everyday, he had several barrels loaded onto his wagon and taken out to the town dump for disposal. If the wind blew away from town, it wasn't so bad but if not, well, you can imagine.

"We were lucky," Yushka continued. "That year we had moved to our new house which was out of range of the problem but the poor people in town had all this added to the misery of a hot dry summer. The people were miserable but not the animals. The smell brought every loose pig and goat by the hundreds to the Plutka feast. I don't know what eating too much pickles would do to a person but what it did to the animals was not pleasant! Fortunately for Chaim, people are forgiving and have short memories. He was also fortunate that a good part of his business was outside of Plutka, so when the circumstances changed, he was back in business. Actually, it worked out well for him. The drought had stopped the flow of his delicacies to his customers, so when he started again, the appetite was there, ready and waiting. His business became better than ever.

"Soon after Chaim's business returned to normal, his family had a meeting and it was decided to move to a city where they could build a factory. The children wanted a home that didn't reek of pickle smells. The children wanted better, more professional lives. What was good for Mom and Pop for generations was not good for them. Those in

Plutka that remembered the dreadful drought were happy to see them leave, most others were not. In any case, the pickle wagons still kept the name with one change. It now read 'Chaim's Plump Plutka Pickles'. Years passed quickly and Chaim handed over the business to his eldest son."

The Mayor arranged for a testimonial in his honor. Chaim agreed. It coincided with his 100th birthday. Yushka had managed to get me an invitation. The crowd filled the hall in the Big Shul. Chaim had made 'Plutka' famous and they were going to show their appreciation. On the dais were all the dignitaries. Chaim, a man the size of a barrel, sat proudly, looking no more than 50. With all that pickle juice in his veins, why not!

Respect

If I say that I have a relative who is a millionaire, you would be shocked. Don't be shocked! I will not swear that he is really a millionaire, but close. Remember, we were talking about invitations on my last visit and would you believe a coincidence, when I got home, there was an invitation waiting for me. Such an invitation I have never seen. Gold lettering on linen paper?

At first, I thought it must be some mistake but then it occurred to me that it must be from a distant relative because no near relative of mine could be that rich. The address was in a place called, "Odessa-by-the-Sea!" At first, I said to myself, 'How stupid! Of course Odessa is by the sea. Where else is Odessa?' Then my dear smart wife said that it must be something like a private section, a special area for the rich. And she was right. It was also she who figured out the connection between us and the distant relative. She decided that we should accept even though I was worried about not fitting in.

"We're not paupers!" she argued. "We are honest Jews and if we get invited, we should go!" So she sent back our acceptance and we prepared our best High Holy Day clothing for the trip. So as not to make it a total loss, I decided to load up my wagon with books and make business stops along the way. Odessa was never a good place to sell books. People go there to enjoy the sun and sea, not to read. And this became more evident later. To tell the truth, I could have saved myself the trouble. I returned with the same books. But that's not the story.

We arrived along with hundreds of other guests. No, I'm not exaggerating! What was amazing was that everything had been arranged for our stay at an exclusive seaside resort. Maybe it was luxury for us but probably not for all those fancy guests that arrived by train or coach. The accommodations were great and the dining hall superb. A note at our table invited us to a tour of the host's home. Excuse me! Mansion! Half of Plutka could fit in the place. At the entrance we stood in awe. Were we in the wrong place? This was certainly the Palace of the Czar! No Jew, not even Rothschild could own such a place. Wherever we faced, there was our image in glass mirrors or polished marble. The walls were covered with tapestry and paintings. Wealth oozed from every room. We thought the hotel was elegant but compared to this, it was mediocre. Nothing was ever mentioned about how this cousin had amassed such wealth and it would have been rude to ask.

The only clue came when we were shown the study. Except for 'French' windows all of the walls were covered with Law Books. All in Russian or French! Not one book in Yiddish or Hebrew. And that was the only place books were seen in the house. Either reading was forbidden or all the books were hidden in storage as though having books was shameful. At the end of the tour, we finally were greeted by the host family. It was then that I saw the resemblance my cousin had to my beloved departed, Great-Uncle Leizer. After a few remarks, his charming wife expressed their wishes for us to feel welcome, to enjoy our visit. Their Simkha. The children looked on in awe at the throng of strangers.

All this was a prelude to the main event. It was a gorgeous Saturday morning that the seaside was known for. The parade of worshipers extended for blocks to the magnificent Temple. What amazed me was the number of men wearing the old traditional costume that I would have expected in the shtetl. The difference was in the quality of fox and sable fur adorning the Shtreimel and coat collars of the men and the mink and lamb coats of the women. The Synagogue was almost full when we arrived although the service had just begun. I cannot describe the elegant moorish structure or the use of marble and gold, for it was breathtaking. The women's galleries hung on three sides above the immense sanctuary. The stained glass dome brightly illuminated the room and gave the cantors voice a powerful resonance.

It also made the business talk of the men congregants audible. One could hardly follow the prayers for the noise. Were it not for the cues from the rabbi, even I would have gotten lost. The din was so great that the Rabbi had to interrupt the Cantor several times to ask for decorum. It subsided for a while, then began again. Then the Torah was taken out for the weekly portion. No sooner had the chanting begun than the chatter increased. I tried to follow the reading in the Khumash/Pentateuch but the reader was hardly audible. When the members of the Bar Mitzvah party were given the honor of being called up to the Torah, one would think some respect would be given but there was no change. I couldn't believe that this was an Orthodox Congregation.

Speaking of respect, an elderly guest was looking for a seat. A man, obviously infirm from the cane he carried. I moved from my seat at the end of the bench to allow him access to sit where he could extend his lame leg. A latecomer from the congregation took a position in the aisle next to the old man and commenced to pray. If it was intentional, I don't know but his backside was right in the face of the old man. I tapped the shoulder of the young man, indicating that he should move back a bit to take his rear out of the old man's face. His response, a snooty rejection. I offered changing places with the guest but he graciously declined. Respect!

Finally, the Bar Mitzvah was called up for the Maftir reading. One would think that this, the highlight of the service would get some respect. The Rabbi had to plead for silence out of regard for the boy whose voice was no match for this noisy congregation. When he began the blessings for the Haftorah reading, the women in the balcony shouted down for the men to be quiet. Where the Rabbi failed, the women succeeded. At least for the duration of the boy's recital. The young man in the aisle finally finished his devotion and moved forward a little, removing his rear end from my neighbor's face. But now he stood completely blocking the platform from which the Bar Mitzvah was chanting. To have traveled all this way, not to see the honoree was very sad. At least, I could hear him. To my chagrin, my wife happily reported she saw and heard perfectly from above. The Kiddush and reception were understandably fabulous. The whole experience, overall, exceptional. Best of all, I was reintroduced to my father's family.

I sent the Bar Mitzvah the gift he needed. "The Complete Works of Sholem Aleikhem."

Gershon Gossip

"I'm sure that the Talmud forbids gossip!" Yushka began as we sat around the sabbath table after a hearty dinner. His dear wife was finishing the dishes and we had completed our Grace After Meals. What had brought out that comment was a story that I had been telling about a woman from a shtetl that I seldom visited on my rounds as a book seller, a town called Dobromil, somewhere in the south of Poland. She was nicknamed "Genendl the Town Clock." Why such a name?" you may ask. Just as Genendl made it her business to know everyone's business, so did the town clock, standing high above, in the steeple of the Town Hall, all four faces constantly watching what went on. I'm sure every town had it's gossip, a woman who made everyone's problems her problems and everyone's joys hers too.

This Genendl, rumor had it, was unusual for a teller of tales. Although she was driven by some unearthly force, she actually was a good woman. "A good woman? A Gossip?" you may wonder. Well, her nosiness often ferreted out difficulties that might have otherwise been hidden. You want a "Such as!" A for instance. When Rivkah, the youngest daughter of the tailor was planning to elope with Yankl, the Yeshiva scholar because they were so in love, Genendl's gossip stopped it cold. No elopement! Neither parents had the money to make a wedding and the lovers couldn't wait. It would have been shameful and a sin had the children done what they intended. When she exposed their secret plans, the whole town got together and groshe by groshe they collected enough to make a wedding for them. Not a big wedding! Not a fancy wedding! But, as you say, "A Kosher Wedding!"

The canopy was set up in the courtyard of the Shul. The wonder of it is, that gossip spreads, evil gossip as much as good gossip. Genendl's words reached as far as Lvov and a klezmer band decided to play for the Bride and Groom, gratis. The Rabbi performed for the payment of a charitable donation. The Bride's father, was so happy that the elopement was canceled, that he sewed a beautiful gown for his daughter. The money that the town collected, helped the young couple get started in their blessed life together.

"Blessed life?" you may ask. Yes! The student soon became a renowned Rabbi. His bride was soon blessed with a baby girl. She was named, "Gittel" in honor of a woman gossip. If not for "Genendl, der Shtut Zeger", none of this would have happened. But she was still ridiculed for being the town gossip. Few people remembered the good she did when it was easier to remember the evil. For the one wedding that she saved, she was responsible for many tragic divorces."

Yushke rose to fill the glasses with hot tea from the Samovar, the look on his face showing his eagerness to tell his own gossip story. But that would have to wait, as the two men sucked the steeping hot tea through the sugar cube clenched between their teeth. The night was wearing on but the two friends were not ready to turn in. The empty glasses were set aside. Yushke began. "His name was "Gershon, Gershon Gossip!"

Immediately, I interrupted. "But Gershon is a man's name! A man gossip?"

"Why not? You never heard of a man gossip? The difference is, a man has an ulterior motive. At first, I had nothing to do with this person. A middle aged man, a stranger who came to our town about the time of the 'Jacket Incident'. Maybe it was in pursuit of the reward money. Who knows? Anyhow, he took a room in the tavern and did business from there. This I heard from the grapevine, so to speak. Where he came from, I have no idea. Someone said that he had been run out of town and there were other stories about him, speculations. And speaking of speculation, that was his business. He was a 'Hondler!' He was always dressed well, even on a weekday, and his good looks and friendly personality were an asset to his wheeling and dealing.

"Wherever two or three men gathered, he became the fourth. He seldom spoke, except to pose a question, a word of encouragement to further the conversation. Often it came to be valuable in his business, often it was just idle talk that ingratiated himself to someone else. Unfortunately, he was not as discreet as he should have been. In many cases, his bit of gossip fell into the wrong hands creating problems. His business took him to other towns where his remarks were deemed offensive. One time, he arrived in Plutka followed by a mob of angry Ukrainians who claimed he not only swindled them but defamed one their daughters. It was a miracle that he didn't get killed or that we didn't suffer a pogrom. I never heard what he had said or done because the town elders were able to pay off the gentiles and send them back home.

"But that was beyond our borders. Here he was constantly busy. As I said, I had no business with the man and had little time or patience with the talk about town. We had our own gossip's, so we didn't need an outsider causing trouble. Soon, everybody became careful of talking important things when Gershon was in earshot. But he was very skilled. He could make a whole Megillah (book) out of nothing. Lifelong friends began to mistrust each other for fear the words said in confidence would get to the 'Gossip'.

Even business deals had to be sworn to secrecy lest Gershon might find out and spread the word.

"The Rabbi was asked for help. Perhaps he could be banned from the Shtetl. Nothing could be done. As I said before, I had no dealings with him. If I met him in the Shul, I greeted him as I would any Jew and he greeted me. From my personal knowledge, none of the talk about him was true. His ready smile and solid handshake belied the evil attributed to him. Yet, I was wary. By the way, at this time, my nephew was away studying mathematics, on a scholarship at the University in Kiev. One friday afternoon, on my way home from Mikvah (Ritual bath), we met. He greeted me warmly as I did him. He said, 'Mazel Tov! I hear your nephew is away in Kiev, studying? Studying what?' Why I said, 'Studying to be a Rabbi!' I don't know why, but I did. Later, as I entered the shul, the Shammas approached me. 'Mazel Tov, Reb Yushka! Your nephew is in Kiev studying to be a Rabbi?' he said. 'Gershon Gossip!' I said and nearly fell down laughing."

Blessed Beryl

A long time ago, I promised to tell you about Beryl, now Boris, the noted singer and concert performer. Please forgive me for the delay but it has taken me this much time to sort out the facts from the fiction. Then again, who can be sure, even today which is which. The only fact that I can affirm is that blind Beryl is no longer blind. This I saw with my own two eyes at the concert.

From what I gathered, the troupe that he left with, did very well. They were in show business, and you know how those people are when it comes to piety. Daily prayer is soon forgotten, strictly kosher food neglected. In other words, they forgo their responsibility. The 613 becomes ten and even most of the ten are forgotten. Never-the-less, the Lord was good to him. Wherever they went, people flocked to hear his magnificent voice. The collection plate overflowed. His romance reached heights one only dreamed of. Now the headliner was "Boris the Magnificent." But he had little other gratification for he was trapped in his black world. His soul mate, gave him love and comfort. She read to him from the literature of the day. She took him to the theater and concerts whenever they were performing in the city. She opened a window for him to the world outside of his shtetl experience. And he absorbed everything.

His muse took him out of his darkness and he began to write music for the show. The audiences were delighted with the new songs which became so popular, one could hear them throughout the country. Words and melodies flowed from his head. He soon had hit songs being performed by other musicians. "The moon is nothing without you!", "The flame in my heart!" and the real heartbreaker, "If only I could see your love!" Of course they were written in Yiddish and when it was publicized that he was the composer, translations appeared in Russian, making his audiences even greater and more diverse The klezmer band grew to become a concert orchestra, outdoor performances gave way to halls and theaters. Boris became a bonanza.

One time, at one of his klezmer performances, a teacher of classical singing approached him and offered him an opportunity to study opera. This would mean having to limit his contact with the Klezmer but they encouraged him to pursue the study. They even paid his tuition. This instructor would be one of many to undertake the training of Boris' magnificent voice. Everything would have been fine, except that he was lonely. He missed the warm comradeship of the musicians, the love of his nightingale. He missed the warmth of his adoring audiences. His training was rigorous and he was protected from any distraction. He had no one to read to him. His head was so full of the scores of others that he no longer wrote his own.

At first, letters from the troupe were frequent but after a while they became sparse and then rare. The amorous notes from his love, soon became impersonal. He realized what a terrible price he had to pay for his choice. Then the time arrived when he was ready to perform. A stage was contracted for and a solo concert arranged. So much time had passed that the name "Beryl" was no longer remembered and the people who would come to the classical performance that he was to give had never heard of his life with the klezmer.

It was a disaster! No sooner did he appear with an usher leading him to the piano on stage than a murmur rose from the audience. They could not appreciate his fantastic voice or skill because of the distraction due to his blindness. He could feel the cold coming over the footlights and it affected his singing. The joy he felt when singing with the klezmer was missing. He decided then and there not to continue this life. He realized that this world was not for him even though the critics were kind. He did not regret the experience nor the time and effort but he did regret the loneliness and sterility of this life. "Perhaps if he were not blind, things would have been different!" he thought. With sincere apologies he left and returned to his home in Plutka.

Some wise man said, "Time changes all things!" By the time Beryl had returned, things were quite different. Not only had he grown up, the town did also. There was now a big synagogue where the old shul had stood and the congregation had tripled. Not since he had left had their been a Cantor. No one could equal the chanting that Beryl had brought to the services. As though the job had been held for him, Beryl was hired. Again, for the first time in a long time, he was happy. Not as happy as when he was with the klezmer, but happy. It all came back to him, the liturgy, the music and the terrain. The terrain was the hardest because the architecture created hazards he had to learn to negotiate. There were steps leading from the dais where the Arc was that held the Torah scrolls. And there were steps to the platform where the praying and reading table were. Even the path in between had to be measured and negotiated step by step.

Beryl learned this very well and became comfortable in his surroundings. The Congregation was ecstatic! The town was ecstatic! Beryl was happy! As it is said, "God works in mysterious ways!" They even called him, "Blessed Beryl" (No evil eye!) And that's where my story begins! It was on the evening of our joyful celebration, "Simkhat Torah" and the scrolls were being passed from one man to another to be carried around the synagogue, to be danced with. Suddenly, a cry of terror shattered the joyful noise. Beryl holding the largest Torah in his arms had made a misstep or tripped on his tallis and had fallen to the floor. The miracle was that he landed on his back with the Torah in his arms above him. God forbid the tragedy of the scroll falling to the floor. Immediately, the men removed the Torah to safety. Beryl lay unconscious, having struck his head on the step as he fell, trying to prevent the Torah dropping to the floor.

The doctor ordered his removal to the city hospital. The holiday joy continued. The congregation was happy that they were spared the penitence prescribed for the desecration of the Torah. Beryl lay in the hospital. Thanks to God, he awoke the next day. The doctor was called to witness the miracle. You may ask, "The miracle that he came out of the coma?" Well that, too! The miracle that he was able to see. Blurry at first, but see! Was it a miracle, a gift from God or the result of the fall? What does it matter? Blind Beryl was blind no more!

The Cry Of A Wolf

Whether the weather is controlled by God or has its own mind, is a debate I try to avoid. Especially when I am a guest in someone's home, which I often am. As a seller of books, who travels all around, I am beholden to the righteous who make a safe haven for me, especially on the Sabbath. Although I started out with Holy books, I soon found a market for Hebrew secular poetry and prose, which as you know, soon blossomed into the Golden Age of Yiddish Literature. With the growth of literacy among the Non-Jews, I expanded my business threefold. This took me into areas that a Jew might find disconcerting. Still, being a man of modern persuasion, and a believer in the good Lord's protection, I felt that the opportunity was greater than the threat. Even though, I always had in mind that this was Cossack country, and one cannot be too wary. This was how the conversation started. Yushka and I had finished the Sabbath dinner and settled down to chat while his dear wife cleaned the food and dishes from the table. Usually, it was Yushke who began the conversation but tonight I was the one. There was a light snow and although it was not deep, everything became white.

Yushke offered me the pungent tobacco, then took a deep sniff from his snuff box. We both let go a sneeze, in unison! It almost extinguished the Sabbath candles but it cleared the sinuses as nothing else could do. "I love the snow!" he began. "Not the deep heavy snow but what you might call a dusting. Nothing clears the air better!"

I suggested, not to contradict him but to extend his thought, "A spring shower?"

He agreed and I continued. I explained that many of my Yiddish clientele had become avid readers of the Russian literature. Everything was in Yiddish translation, though many preferred reading the original text. No doubt Tolstoy was favorite, with Dostoyevsky a close second. But the Ukrainians had their own favorites as well and I found it difficult to find those copies to sell. You are aware that my policy was to buy back the books after they were read, at a reduced price, of course. This made my clientele happy, for it was not practical to accumulate books or have library space in their small homes and shacks and it encouraged them to buy other books with the trade-in money. On my part, it kept my supply full without having to purchase new copies of old books. As the old proverb says, "Reading a book does not wear out the print!" These winter months gave the readers more time away from business and chores. More leisure, so to speak.

"And being snowbound made a good book a fine companion!" Yushka added.

Yushka's wife set two cups of tea, hot from the samovar, before us. The toasty cookies were perfect, after dipping them into the tea. She took a chair near the kerosene lamp to catch up on the mail. Mail from America, the golden land. The envelopes were written in English but the letters were written in 'Mama Lushen,' (mother tongue) Yiddish. These letters always brought tears to her eyes, not that the content was sad but that she missed her family that had gone away. We pretended not to notice, so as not to embarrass her. Every so often, she would interrupt with, "Sh'mil sends a 'greess'(regards) or Malke sends her love."

I also got letters from America. They would all be stacked up waiting for my return. Some had good news, some not so good. The winter snows in New York, they tell me, are just as bad as here and they have no fireplaces in their buildings, so they have to shlep pails of coal up seven flights for the stove. But that has nothing to do with a wolf.

It didn't look threatening when I started out but toward noon, snowflakes as big as my fist began to fall. I urged my horse to trot, hoping to reach some sort of settlement, deep in the Ukrainian hinterland. The falling snow blinded me and blinded my horse. The road disappeared as everything on all sides became one immense white field. There were no trees to guide us. Nothing! For all I know we were riding in a circle. I began to panic! The wagon refused to follow the horse and the horse was beginning to skid. I undid the reins and left the wagon, believing I could lead the horse to a safe place. Soon the snow was too deep for me, so I mounted the horse, urging him forward, what I thought was forward.

Then, off in the distance, I heard a noise. I stopped to listen. Carried by the wind it sounded like a dog or maybe a wolf. I thought, if it was a dog, it had to have a master who had to have a home, shelter. If it was a wolf...trouble! A hungry wolf, in a pack, in this wilderness was not such a good thing! My horse smelled danger and I had to urge him on, even at our peril. 'Owooo!" The closer we got, the clearer the message. It was definitely a wolf. But it sounded like just one wolf, not a pack. Then I remembered having heard that Ukrainian peasants often keep a wolf for protection. The "Owooo!" seemed to be getting closer. Now, I got off my horse who was balking, refusing to go on. I had to take the reins and pull the beast forward against his will. I never thought that I would beg a beast, but I did. I promised him all kinds of rewards. You wouldn't believe it, it worked. Still hesitating, he seemed to get his courage and we moved toward the howling wolf, through the howling blizzard.

My hunch was right. I could make out the gray silhouette of a peasant's hut. 'Blessed be the Almighty!' I kept saying. My horse kept snorting his, 'Amen!' As we approached, the wolf stopped howling. Instead, it began to growl. A fierce, menacing growl. If it had not been bound with a rope, I probably would have been his dinner. The noise of the wolf must have aroused the man in the house because as we came closer, I could see lights from candles being lit. A small figure dressed in a bearskin opened the door just as we got there and beckoned us in. "Us!" you ask? Yes! Me and my horse. Without a word, he brought out two woolen blankets, one for me and one for my horse. He took up an axe and I thought it was time to say the 'Sh'mah!' He smashed it across a tree trunk, threw several of the logs on the fire and stoked it into a roaring flame. I shivered and so did my horse. A large pot filled with snow was set over the flame. He found an immense knife and approached me, its blade flashing in the firelight. I shut my eyes waiting for the final blow. The blow landed on the loaf of black bread which he cut into fat slices. As I took one he grunted, "Goy! Don't you wash first and make a 'Motzy Lekhem'?" (prayer for bread)

Dr. Seegood

On one visit to Plutka, I noticed a change in Yushka's appearance. It wasn't his beard, or his haircut, it was his eyes. He was wearing eyeglasses! Not only did he have eyeglasses but so did his wife. My question was, "Why?" He began to explain.

"Dr. Seegood had a family special! Two for the price of one! Now, everyone wears glasses! That is everyone that has a problem with his vision. That is everyone who can afford glasses. Just as you go around selling books, some new, some used, so does the eyeglass merchant. Dr. Seegood had a special covered wagon, which housed his office, his testing room and his stockroom. When he came to town, he would park in the square, ring his bell, a deep gong like sound, different from that of other merchants and gather all the people with lures of cures for all their vision problems.

"For those who saw far, he had glasses to make them see near. For those who saw near, he had glasses to make them see far. And for those who saw fuzzy or crooked, he would send away to the big city for corrective lenses. But the big deal was his frames. If you wanted to look studious, like a Talmud student, he had a frame. For a shrewd businessman, he had a frame. He had frames for young and for old. That is, the frame would make a young person look older and an older person look younger. He had frames for people with sick eyes and frames for people with healthy eyes. If you didn't need a lens, he could give you glasses without the glass that made you look like a genius, although everyone might think you were a fool."

"You mean to tell me, all the people bought glasses whether they needed them or not?" I asked. "I wish I could sell books as well as he sold glasses."

"Wait! That wasn't all. He had green glass for people in wintertime and blue glass for summertime wear. If you needed rose colored glasses to cheer you up, he had that too. He set up a little stage where he would call up a man or girl to sample a pair and ask the opinion of the audience. If they disapproved, he would try another pair. Some lucky person would get a pair free. Completely free! His assistant worked inside the wagon, fitting and adjusting the glasses to fit. He even had an exchange policy but by the time you wanted to make a change, he was gone. It seemed that everybody loved Dr. Seegood, everybody except the poor peasants who were jealous of the Jews, even the poor ones. They could never afford those fancy glasses.

"One year, several of the young Ukrainians stormed the wagon and grabbed some of the fanciest glasses for themselves. They put the glasses on as they ran from the square. The police had little trouble catching them because their vision was so impaired by the incorrect lenses that they had taken. They were running into trees and tripping over objects they couldn't see. Well, that was the funniest thing! Almost the funniest thing. After Dr. Seegood packed up and left Plutka, everyone went around town flaunting their miracle glasses. It became a bragging contest, each person trying to outdo the other. Each person making up better stories than Dr. Seegood could ever invent. Except for the one that he had told me in confidence."

I couldn't wait to hear the secret story. Yushka could hardly wait to tell me. But it had to wait. I had to use the outhouse! I never could break away from a good yarn. The chair that I had sat in was still warm when I returned to my position. Yushka hadn't stirred. He began again!

"It happened in a shtetl, the name too hard to pronounce and harder to remember. What wasn't hard was the name of the Rebbe. "Reb Moishe Kalt" He never explained where the name came from but it fit the man to a tee. He was as cold as ice on a frosty day. Study was his middle name. Even on the joyous Sabbath, study preceded prayer and followed prayer. His congregation revered him but the children hated him! For him, there was no room for frivolity. Even food was a frivolity. From the age of three the children were bonded to him and the kheder/school. He never used physical punishment on a wayward child. That he delegated to the father. The father was merciless. The people were poor, near starving for food but not learning.

"The Rebbe believed that one's eternal soul would benefit from a suffering body. The girls were separated from the boys, even in the same family, for fear of evil temptation. He said that Holy books were forbidden to girls so they were tutored in the Yiddish translation of prayer and law. Many were sent to work in households as maids or seamstresses, so they could earn their keep. It was a cruel life, not just a simple life."

"I think I know the place." I interrupted. "I was driven out from such a shtetl, many years ago. I had been warned not to go there but being young and foolish, I decided to take the chance. I thought stoning was nonexistent until I tried to sell my books. But what had all this to do with glasses?"

Yushka waited patiently, always courteous to me, as guest and friend. He went on with the Doctor's story. "You know that in poor Yeshivas, there is a shortage of books, so the children sit across from each other at narrow tables. One boy reads from the book in the right direction as the other boy learns the material by rote. Of course, there are boys that are able to learn to read upside down but that is exceptional.

Each week, the book is turned around so that the other boy gets a chance to read right side up. This system has been used for years and apparently has worked. Great scholars have come from such a setting with no sign of deprivation. Great Rabbis have known this system. So this Rebbe saw no problem with it.

"Then Dr. Seegood came up with a plan. He made a new pair of glasses with special lenses. Instead of glasses that corrected distance, he made glasses that inverted the image. He arranged a visit with Rebbe Moishe and offered these glasses free of charge. The Rebbe agreed to test them. A boy tried them out. The result was unbelievable. The upside down letters righted themselves The test proved successful! It was a miracle! If only the Rebbe would buy a pair for each child the Doctor knew he would become a millionaire. The Rebbe turned him down because new books would have cost less than the special glasses. I bought the formula! And I need a partner to become a millionaire." Yushka sat waiting for my answer. Was he putting me on? Or what?

The Bells

I'm sure you remember, the blacksmith. I told you about Yank'l, the tavern, the Rabbi, a while back. Well, Yank'l had become a model in the community. The Rabbi, not to speak evil, did enjoy the tavern once in a while but not the blacksmith. And God was good to him! His business blossomed and he hired many men to work for him. All day long you could hear the chorus of hammer on anvil. His reputation spread all over the country and jobs kept coming in. I don't mean small jobs. I mean projects. I'm sure you know that churches need steeples and steeples need bells. For some strange reason there was a resurgence of religious fervor in the Ukraine, not good for the Jews but very good for Yank'l. He had moved his shop out to the edge of town where land was cheap and there he built not just a shop but a foundry. "What's a foundry?" A foundry is a blacksmith shop, only bigger! Much bigger! Bigger forges! Bigger anvils and bigger hammers. All of a sudden the town became quiet. Everyone found out that what had been normal conversation was shouting. How could one hear one another over the 'klopping and hocking' from Yank'l's place. The silence was deafening! The banging used to start at sunrise and end after dark. The bad thing, the din never stopped. The good thing was that the Jewish men were roused from their sleep by the noise, to attend morning prayer Now everyone overslept, to the peril of their eternal souls.

The foundry did wonders for the shtetl. Because jobs arrived from far and wide, business improved. The tavern was enlarged to accommodate the strangers' needs and soon the inn was made larger for overnight lodging. Transients were wealthy, so the merchants enjoyed new business. The main street changed. New enterprises grew up and old ones grew larger. There was talk of building a new and larger synagogue for a younger Rabbi. Money was collected to pave the muddy street. The money paved someone's bank account but not the street. But that's another story!

And speaking of the synagogue, the biggest donor was Mr. Yank'l. Now, the shameful term 'blacksmith' was omitted from his name. The old shul would remain, it was decided. The old Rabbi would remain, too. The daily prayers would be held there for the old timers who remained very orthodox. The yeshiva for little boys didn't change, except for one thing. In a fit of generosity, one of Yank'l's patrons gave money so that every child would have his own books. That he was the publisher of 'Loshon Kodesh Inc.' (holy language) may have had something to do with it.

If you think all this prosperity went to their heads, believe me, you're right! Everyone did well! Everyone would except me. "Why?" you may ask. "Didn't their good fortune allow them time and money for books?" All that was true except that an enterprising couple from Roumania saw the opportunity and opened "The Plutka Book Shoppe" and stocked it with literature from all over the world. No used or worn copies. All brand new and with the new prosperity, the people could afford the luxury. On my latest trip, I screwed up my courage and visited the 'Shoppe' and was shocked to find tables and chairs for the people to sit and browse. I took a seat near the window, pretending to glance through a book when the young proprietress approached and asked in her sweet Roumanian Yiddish, if I would like a glass of tea or coffee while I waited to buy a book. "A tea!" I replied, a little embarrassed for I had no intention of buying a book. "So this was my competition!" I thought. How could my horse and wagon compete? Not here in Plutka, anymore. I finished my tea and decided to leave but I couldn't leave empty handed. I picked up the latest copy of short stories by my favorite author, Sholem Aleikhem, hot off the press.

I headed straight to Yushka's place to tell him what had happened.

"See what happens when you stay away for a long time!" It was true. It had been several years. What with illness and other 'tsurus'(trouble), I had been unable to travel. Then he started to tell me about everything that happened since I had been here last. About the changes, as I told you above, the prosperity, everything that all started because Yank'l built a foundry.

"You understand that the Jewish community thrived but the Non-Jewish community did as well. Usually, it works in reverse, but not in Plutka. It was once a haven for Jews, a traditional shtetl but as the saying goes, 'Nothing remains the same on God's good earth!' We never had a church but we do now! We never had a priest but we do now! Maybe the good Lord, in his wisdom has given us these things to protect us from the crazy Cossacks. Who knows? Anyhow this priest who would one day be a Bishop, decided not to build just a church, it had to be a Cathedral. After all it was in competition with our new synagogue.

"This Cathedral was immense. Our new synagogue could fit inside it with room to spare. The priest brought masons from all over and stained glass artists from Czechoslovakia. The town was flooded with workers from all over Europe. He would be the envy of everyone in the church, even the Pontiff himself. For just a priest to undertake such a project was unheard of. But he had been advised of his pending elevation in the church and was just getting prepared. The hierarchy certainly approved, for it was their money that was making it possible. The steeples would be immense, their spires reaching to the heavens.

The bells had to sound spectacular. There were the greatest foundries in France and Germany, with reputations going back to the middle ages. But it was Yank'l who was given the job. Yank'l who had never rung a bell, no less built one. He was an iron worker, he insisted. He never worked with brass or bronze. But the priest ordered it be done and it had to be done. Yank'l the Jew could not refuse.

"Yank'l hired bell specialists. He bought the materials they needed and the different molds for different tones. All other jobs had to wait! Special kilns had to be built The bells had to be installed for the Mass on Christmas Eve. The stress should have driven him back to drink, especially when the priest hounded him daily with his taunts, "Jew this! Jew that! Remember this! Remember that!" He even threatened not to pay one ruble if the timbre wasn't perfect.

"Just before Christmas and coincidentally Chanukah, the bells were installed and tested. They were arranged to play a special hymn. At midnight the bells rang out! "Ma'oz Tzur Yeshuasi!" (favorite Jewish Chanukah hymn)

Town of Tlit

Speaking of happy holidays, I'm reminded of the year that I happened to be in Plutka just in time to celebrate Purim with my dear friend Yushka. No doubt you know the whole Megilla (scroll) about Esther and Mordekhai, so I'm not going to rehash all of that but as is our tradition, actually a Mitzvah, to get tipsy. Understand, we didn't overdo it, just enough to be happy, silly shiker. It was after the Purim feast, also an obligation, that we were having tea and his wife's delicious Human Tashen, those three corner fruit filled pastries, also a special Purim treat, that Yushka blurted out, "Did I ever tell you about the town of Tilt?"

Without waiting for my reply he began. It took a little effort for him to focus, then he said, "Remember the story you told me about Lisp? Well, this is about a town called 'Tilt'. "Why Tilt?" you may ask because.... Let me start at the beginning. You know that our people lived in western Europe after the expulsion from Spain in 1492. Then the rulers under the church's edicts threw us out and we migrated eastward to Galitzia, Russia and so on. There was a small group, actually an extended family who wandered for many years looking for the ideal place to settle and finally they found it somewhere in the Carpathian mountains. The patriarch was a very beloved and learned Rebbe, maybe you've heard of him, Rebbe Yonah of Carpathia.

"Crossing the mountains was a great hardship but he urged his followers on, promising them the promised land and suddenly from the top of Mount Nebo, it appeared. Between two high mountains lay a beautiful valley with a beautiful stream flowing between them. "God be praised!" he shouted. "Here is our Jordan! We will make our Jerusalem on this hill, until the Messiah brings us back to the real Jerusalem." With singing and dancing the group descended into the valley and began the job of building their new home. They never questioned why such an idyllic place hadn't been settled before. Trees were hewn, homes were built and planting was begun.

"Everything was going great until the spring rains filled the banks of the stream and it became a river. The floods washed all the homes away and the people had to scramble up the mountain to safety. The Rebbe gathered his flock around him and they thanked God for sparing them. No sooner than the rains stopped than they began building again, but this time up the side of the mountain. Not as easy as you might think. The angle of the mountain was very steep and they had to design their homes and their lives to accommodate the situation.

"Every home had to be built on a slant. Even the synagogue had to be built on a slant. Overcoming this condition was much harder than you think. Although the walkways were leveled off, navigating the mountain was hazardous and difficult. The Rebbe in his wisdom, told the cobbler to raise the sole on one foot so as to equalize the balance. The only problem came when one wanted to go in the opposite direction But that was a minor consideration. The adults made the supreme effort to cope and the Rebbe was there to encourage them.

"The children had thought it was fun but when they played and dropped a toy or ball, it would roll down the mountain and had to be chased all the way to be retrieved. It was decided to set out barriers to catch a falling object and it worked very well.

"How did I come to hear about this story? One day, years ago, a man hobbled into my shop. I thought he might have been crippled until he explained that because of his town on the side of a mountain, one shoe was higher than the other. I suggested that he get one pair of shoes for flat places like Plutka and he was indebted to me for life. When I asked what the name of the town was, he answered, "Why, Tilt of course!" Who thought of that name? I asked. "The Rebbe, of course." And that made sense, since everything was tilted.

"Every so often, he came to Plutka and never failed to give me a good order. I never got to ask him how the people managed with transportation. One day he volunteered the information. In Tilt itself there was no need, except for wheelbarrows or carts. Incoming materials were hoisted down from the top of the mountain on wooden rails. Life was hard but satisfactory. The fertile valley fed them well and except for minor problems the Tiltians were happy. Then catastrophe struck."

Fresh tea was poured and more Human Tashen served. "What happened?" I asked.

"Nature is a capricious master! The town of Tilt suffered landslides, snow slides, mud slides and still survived. But they never expected what came at them. The winter was especially brutal. The snowfall exceeded any in history. When the spring thaw came the flood waters rose so high, the entire town was uprooted. The people fled to the mountain top and were saved. The Rebbe told them that God had promised never to drown the people as he did at the time of Noah. They watched helplessly as their homes and synagogue was swept into the powerful water. They expected everything to be washed away except for a miracle. The center of the flood waters developed a whirlpool which tossed every building around and around in a circle. As the water receded, it set all the buildings down on the opposite mountain, exactly in the same position as it was in Tilt. Even the synagogue landed facing the east. The Rebbe fell to his knees and prayed the prayer of thanks.

"In time the flood again became a stream. The people moved across to the other side and set up their homes, again. The slope was the same but reversed. The angle of the buildings had to be reversed. Even the soles of the shoes, reversed. Actually, except for the rising and falling of the heavenly bodies, everything was the same. The people went about their business as before. The planting took place and the harvest was successful. The children had to adjust their play and the adults, their lives to accommodate the change. The transition was difficult but the Rebbe's encouragement made it easier, after all, he kept saying, "It's the will of God!" And so it was!"

I sat there amazed. I don't know whether it was the Purim wine or the story but Yushka was never better in his telling a story. I just sat there, afraid to speak. Yushka added one thing.

"One thing more needed changing. All the people agreed with the Rebbe, if everything was now reversed, the name had to be as well. It was changed to, 'TLIT!'"

Words of Wisdom

The friend that I met at the Bar Mitzvah, as I mentioned above, has kept up a correspondence all these years and I looked forward to each of his letters as I did visiting Yushka in Plutka. Actually, it was after the services that it started with a vitz, a joke about himself.

He said, "Have you heard this one? 'A deaf man heard a mute man tell him that a blind man saw a crippled man running up a flat mountain?"

I don't know whether he was trying to teach me something or was just joking but above each letter, he wrote a yiddish proverb. During my illness, I rewrote them in a collection that I have shared with Yushka and now with you. It may lose a little ta'am (flavor) in the translation. Enjoy!

Getting in is always easier
than getting out.
In joy, a year is like a day,
in sorrow a day is like a year.
A bitter heart talks a lot.
A smack is forgotten but
a word is forever.
A liar isn't believed even
when he tells the truth.
A liar listens to his own lies
as long as he believes them.

When there is a cure for an illness
it is a half-illness.
Better to have small buns of your own
than a stranger's whole bread.
Don't eat the noodles before the fish.
The truth can go naked but
a lie must be dressed.
He who sees his own foolishness
is wise.
A fool goes into the tub
to wash his face.

Sometime the cure is
worse than the disease.
What good is it that a horse
cost a penny, if you don't
have a penny.
The ears must hear what
the mouth says.
Money that can change a pauper
can change a mentsh.
Overcoming trouble is good to tell.
Trouble with soup is better than
trouble without soup.
If someone saves a person it is a
though he has saved the world
If the bride can't dance
the musicians are at fault.
Better to be alone
than be with fools.
If you have a baby in the carriage
you must let people gloat.
Because of a bad experience
good people suffer.
Busy hands bring an end to work.
When the ordained arrives
no two words are needed.
On miracles we must not rely.
Don't put off for tomorrow
what you can manage today.
Youth is a problem, manhood a
struggle and old age, regret.

One cries for the dead seven days,
for a fool all his life.
A man isn't married until he
understands every word that
his wife doesn't say.
He who seeks a friend without faults,
will be friendless.
Better to light one candle than
curse the darkness.
Personality surpasses beauty.
Better a dry piece of bread with love
than a feast without love.
If you play with a cat you
must learn how to scratch.
A fool falls on his rear
and bruises his nose.
Before the reward of happiness
one's soul could depart.
Sometimes it is more important
for people than for G-d.
Small children don't let you sleep
grown children don't let you rest.
Better silence than gossip.
Better a crumb in silence
than a meal with argument.
A lot of songs but few noodles.
Better good in a cup than
trouble in a pot.
One chops the wood and
the other groans.

Boy In A Box

As you may have noticed, I haven't talked about the Town of Lisp in a long time, and with good reason. There was little news of importance from there until recently when I ran into an old friend from that town. After some small talk he began to sigh. He went on to explain.

"As you know," he began, "Lisp was one of the places where Jews were not only tolerated but respected. All of a sudden, complete chaos! A child of school age was missing. MISSING! And who are the main suspects? The Jews! Even though it was no where near Passover, the rumors spread. It surely looked like the Jew haters were preparing for a pogrom. Every Jewish home was searched! Every business! Strangers coming into town and going out of town were suspect. Lisp, once a safe haven for our brothers and sisters had become the opposite"

"What happened?" I interrupted, eager to hear what happened.

"It all happened because of the lisp! If you recall, the prince had a lisp and everyone had to talk that way in order to save him from embarrassment. Well, then came Dmytri! Dmytri Petrov. He was a beautiful little boy, perfect in every respect except one. He couldn't talk with a lisp. Just as the little prince had a lisp, little Dmytri couldn't.

From infancy he was expected to learn how. The poor little child was unable! This was very disturbing to everyone. His mother had tried all different tricks to get him to lisp. She tied his tongue with a string but that didn't work. He was offered rewards, candy and cookies to no avail. The family kept him locked away at home, for fear the word would get out to the police that he was a non-lisper, as you know a crime in that town.

"Although his father could ill afford it, they hired a tutor. The man worked for months, all day long. The boy would practice way into the night with no success. Finally, at the age of five, he began a little lisp but the next day he had lost it. They approached their priest to get him to ask for God's help. He sprayed Holy Water in the child's mouth and they lit candles to all the Saints but nothing helped. Their family had lived in this very place for hundreds of years and now everything was in jeopardy because their son couldn't lisp."

"If I remember the Midrash about our Great Rabbi Moses who became a lisper when he burned his tongue. Didn't anyone think of that?"

"Sure they did but no one dared to suggest hurting the child. The father took Dmytri to a doctor in the big city. A speech specialist. He examined and tested and probed and checked. Hours later, he declared, "The patient is perfect. He has no speech impediment what-so-ever." When the doctor was told that that was the problem, he couldn't believe it. He could perform surgery to create the lisp but that was dangerous and very expensive. Dmytri's father could not afford it. Besides it would be irreversible.

"The doctor suggested getting a speech therapist and recommended one in the area near Lisp. The poor boy was in for more torture. He was given hot pepper, hot spices, herbs of all sorts. All kinds of evil tasting liquid potions were forced on him to gargle and swish around his tongue.

"It was a miracle that the sweet child remained sane. He loved his parents so much that he suffered all of these torments. There was one more option that they hadn't tried. The local Gypsy. Some said that she was a witch. In any case, she was summoned to the Petrov home. They told her what the problem was and she reached out her hand. Once money was exchanged, she began with an examination of the boy's hands. She took several amulets from her bag and swung them over the child's head making incantations. When she finished, she ordered the boy to speak.

"Mmmmama! Mmmmama!" the boy cried out.

"Every word he said he stuttered. Stuttered but no lisp. The Gypsy was told to get rid of the stutter and get a lisp but she could not. Dmytri's father threw her out of the house. The stuttering, fortunately was only temporary, brought on by the child's fright. Soon he was back to his perfectly normal self."

"So what has this to do with a pogrom?" I impatiently asked.

"Wait!" he responded. "After all of this the boy started school. Except for some occasional teasing from the class bully, everything was fine. His first teacher adored him. He was good! He was smart! He was beautiful! In the second grade things changed. This teacher took pains to ridicule him for his speech. Soon, all the children in his class began to mimic his speech. The teacher would make him stand and repeat each and every 'th' sound. When he couldn't change the 'S' sound, the children laughed. The teacher thought Dmytri was being obstinate, was mocking him and the switch would be used. The child refused to cry and hid the fact that he was being punished from his parents. Obviously, this affected him emotionally and his grades began to suffer.

"He thought of ways to escape. He could not go on this way. Dmytri decided to skip school, permanently! He left home in the morning, as usual but did not go to school. He found perfect hiding places. He decided to run away, to leave Lisp. He packed a bag with food and would stow away in a box. Something was always being shipped by train in a box. When his parents saw that he hadn't returned from school and was missing, they assumed that the Jews had kidnapped him. And why not? Everyone knew what Jews did to little Christian boys! A search went on! The frustration increased as the hunt proved unsuccessful. Angry mobs began to form. If the boy wasn't found by the next evening, all the Jewish homes would burn.

"Meanwhile, Dmytri sat in a box in the railway station waiting to be loaded onto a train. There he remained until two men came and hoisted him and the box onto a wagon. The box he had hidden in was delivered to the principal's office in the school. Dmytri and the school supplies! When the Principal heard his story he ordered that no further harassment against him would be tolerated. The town celebrated his safe return and the innocent Jews were spared. When this whole story reached the Prince, now a young man, he rescinded the lisping law, forever."

The Plutka Press

It was Yushka who brought up the subject. The talk around town was that it was an embarrassment to our town not have a newspaper. Of course, there were newspapers from Kiev, Odessa, other cities. There were Yiddish papers, Russian papers, a Zionist paper written in Hebrew, even a paper from far away Galitzia. But none actually from Plutka. "If we could have a foundry, a big synagogue and a cathedral with bells, how come we don't have a newspaper?" The word spread around town that we must have a newspaper.

A meeting was called and the what, where and how was decided. What was going to be the cost? Where was the money coming from? How was it going to be paid for? Each entrepreneur would put in a share and the rest of the community would pay a subscription fee according to his means. "Sounds good? Well not as good as it sounds." Everyone agreed that such an enterprise needed a collector, what you call an editor. It also needed a collector, what you call a reporter and most of all it needed a collector to collect the money After a heated debate, Mendl Miser was chosen to handle the money business. If anyone could get a ruble's worth out of a grushe, he could. And trustworthy, like no other.

I asked Yushka, "Why did such a small town need a newspaper when you had Gershon Gossip?"

Yushka let out a big laugh. "Precisely! He was going to be the star reporter!" No one in the world was better suited to the job. He was so happy to be chosen that he offered his services free of charge. All he wanted was to have his name under the headline. To show the confidence of the community, he was also made the secretary, so the minutes of the meeting would be in the first edition. Although the meeting lasted way into the night, everyone left with the satisfaction that the world was going to see Plutka as a name on the map, a place with its own newspaper. A newspaper about Plutka, by Plutkans, for Plutkans. 'The Plutka News' would be its name, everyone agreed."

"And how did it go?" I asked.

At first it was terrific! Everyone was very enthusiastic about it. Gershon was doing a great job, a job he was born to do. People were willing to tell him things that they wanted printed in the paper. Things like upcoming weddings, Bar Mitzvahs, success stories, things like that. There was even a column devoted to advice to the lovelorn, something never thought of in Plutka, something copied from the Kiev papers. It became so popular that a special column was included called, 'The Rabbi Says', full of words of wisdom that no one knew he had. He was so pleased with the response that he began to write sermons of the week, etc. The editor soon had more material for the paper than the original two pages that were planned.

"There was one catch. Plutka had no printer and no press and it couldn't support one. Someone who had business in Kiev had to volunteer to make the delivery of the copy to the printer and arrange for someone else bring the finished printed paper back for distribution.

"At best, this took one week, sometimes two. With all the planning, this was unforeseen. Now, you understand, Plutkans are a humble people. They are patient! They are even tolerable but week old news is not news. An emergency meeting was called about this problem. Should they arrange for a carrier to be responsible for bringing the copy to Kiev? Should they hire someone to travel to Kiev to bring the printed paper back to Plutka as soon as it was ready? The town of Plutka certainly deserved better service."

"So what did they do?" I shouted,

"What do you think? They changed the name from 'Plutka News' to 'Plutka Press!' That way, if the reports were not so new, it didn't matter. Besides, Gershon couldn't keep a secret, as you know. By the time the copy left for Kiev, everyone knew everything. And speaking of Gershon

Gossip, our star reporter, he took his job very seriously. Soon, under his name, there appeared items that had not been exactly volunteered. Stories that were told in confidence seemed to appear after the magic words, 'An anonymous source reports...' or 'Overheard in the Mikvah'. You can well imagine the results.

"For some, this gossip was wonderful but for the object of the gossip it certainly was not. The offended soon stopped buying the paper. The Offender, Gershon, was threatened with retaliation. What was ordinary animus for a small town soon developed into a serious case of pure hatred. No one dared to speak to him or each other. The printed word was too dangerous. Talk could be forgiven, even forgotten, not ink. The Rabbi also came under attack."

"So they called a meeting!" I mockingly interrupted.

"Right!" Yushka replied, laughing. "A meeting! Well, more like a riot! Everyone was shouting. Everyone was accusing the other for spreading the malicious lies and gossip. If Gershon would not have been told... how would he have known? When the editor got up to speak, he could hardly be heard. Finally, he restored order. He made a speech sympathizing with those who were maligned. He reported that the big city newspapers had picked up the story about the Plutka Press and we had succeeded in getting recognition. We were finally on the map! Wasn't that what we wanted, after all!

"The floor was opened for complaints, suggestions. Some of the complaints were valid, most were not. The truth was not to be denied. The biggest problem was that by the time the paper arrived in Plutka, the so called news was not. Only the gossip was hot! In fact, too hot! The meeting broke up when promises were made to eliminate 'harmful or malicious' gossip. The Rabbi, was certainly in favor of that. He also agreed to prepare his column in advance so that when it arrived it would be more current. Gershon was admonished to be more discreet.

The next addition arrived and there were no complaints heard. Everyone was satisfied with the reports and items. The Plutka Press was finally acceptable! For school children! Not adults! Most people took the paper and folded it into their pocket. Soon, the Plutka Press folded, too!"

A Pack of Poems

I'm sure that I mentioned that when my dear friend Yushka became, well, wealthy, he moved from his small house to the outskirts of town. It was just before the Passover cleaning that he came across a packet of poems, hidden up in the attic. It was high up on a beam, obviously secreted there by the writer. The previous owner had moved to the "City of Light!" Yes, Paris and had left no forwarding address. In time, Yushka's curiosity won out and he took the packet down.

From what Yushka had told me, the former owner had a son, Joshua, a brilliant, handsome young man. With the father's wealth, he planned that his son would become a doctor, no less. He had arranged tuition at the famous Hôpital National De Medicine in Paris. The son had successfully passed all the requirements and would even get in under the quota set for Jews. The family was ecstatic over the future and the student was about to graduate from the Yeshiva when the worse thing happened. The young man fell in love with a beautiful girl. From the name on the poetry, the girl was Hannah. As Yushka went on with the story, my mind wandered to the subject of poetry.

I did not carry many books of poetry because there were few at the time and most of my clients had little interest or time for such foolishness. FOOLISHNESS! Not my words but theirs. I love poetry! In fact, every devout Jew reads poetry in his daily prayers. Poems by Moses our Rabbi, King David and his son, King Solomon. In more recent times the works of Chaim Nakhman Bialik are printed in Hebrew, Yiddish and in America, even in English. Most people who adore the stories of Sholem Aleikhem don't realize that he authored some great poetry. I must admit that I am guilty of not pursuing the vast material of Jewish poets as I should, works by Rosenfeld, Maledovsky and the Mladeks.

Truth is, that during the Golden Age of Spain, the Jews were very prolific writers of poetry. Some of our greatest rabbis wrote odes to God, love poems, even bawdy pieces. There are works written in Aramaic, Hebrew, Arabic and Ladino. A whole library could be filled with these books. Sad to say, none of these get the respect they deserve, especially when the teachers and rabbis in the Yeshivas find them wasteful. And speaking of wasteful, that is probably what the boy's father angrily shouted about his son's frivolous writing of poetry.

How did Yushka know that I had been hearing him but not listening to him. Perhaps it was the glazed look in my eyes or the lack of the "Uh! Huh!" that I usually say to indicate that I was paying attention. He graciously waited until I had mentally returned, before he continued.

"Hannah was a very beautiful girl, something that her poor clothes could not hide. She was kind and her deep voice sent shivers through his entire body. He knew that she was his Eve, his Rachel, his Bas Shevah. The words of love that he had memorized from the "Song of Songs" would begin and end with her name, Hannah. When he sat over the G'morrah, her smile would appear among the words. Her image followed him wherever he went, his heart cried out to her. Was it his imagination or the devil's trick that signaled her desire for him. The only release for the pain in his heart was to write his feelings in poetry to her."

"And you have those poems? You've read them, I assume!" I interrupted.

"Would you like to hear some? Yushka offered. "Perhaps a sampling."

"If the Holy one, blessed be He,
Would have seen your face,
He would have had no need
To create the Sun, Moon or Stars."

"Only for one like you, Hannah,
Could Solomon have written
Those immortal love poems.
Only for you, can I!"

"You must realize that there is something lost in the translation. But it is quite obvious that he was well versed. Excuse the pun. Understand that these are only the opening stanzas. Each poem was written on letter paper, addressed to Hannah. He took great pains for his father not to know when he wrote them or posted them. As time went on, he became more obsessed with his love of her and the intensity showed in his words. If Hannah felt the same way, she must have tried to hide it."

"Can the hands of time run faster
To bring us to the heavenly canopy
Where God's blessing will unite us
As with Abraham, Isaac and Jacob."

"Only death, terrible death
Can keep our preordained
Destiny, which binds our souls
From the nuptials of our love."

Yushka finished reading and handed the pack to me. I rifled through the pages, separated from their envelopes. The address was plain to see and the postage paid for and cancelled. This was certainly a mystery to me. Had Hannah returned the poems? Had she rejected his love? How did all of these letters end up atop the beam in the attic? Did the family moving to Paris have anything to do with it?

"All these questions!" Yushka exclaimed. "What I am about to say is based only on guesswork. No sooner than word was out that the house was for sale, and I might say, at a very good price, than I began arrangements to buy it. The agreement was quickly settled, it appeared that the father was anxious to get out as soon after Joshua's graduation from the Yeshiva as possible. I thought that I knew all about the affairs of the people of Plutka but not this family. If the walls could only talk!"

"What about the love letters. What about the poems you found in the attic?" I begged.

"After I found the packet of envelopes, I went over to the post office. The postmaster refused to answer my questions at first. When he recognized Joshua's letters, he told me that the father had ordered the mail be held from delivery. It was the father who had hidden the collection in the attic!"

Foolishness!

I can't remember a more pleasant, warm spring day. I was on my third horse. He was the smartest of them all, and a good thing, too, because at this stage in my life, I would nod off. If it was the warm weather or my age, I can't say. It became very hard for me to read while travelling, not as it used to be. I was headed to Plutka, only a short distance from Brodna. The road was straight and smooth, so I tied the reins to the pole and trusted in the Lord to guide us safely to Yushka's home. As you remember, my visits to Plutka had become social, no longer business since the book store opened. From a distance, I could see the smoke puffing from the foundry chimneys. Plutka was a busy city by now, but still a small city. The main street was paved and homes now filled side streets. It seemed odd, as we passed through town that all of the signs on the shops were in Ukrainian Cyrillic and all the Jewish names were gone. I pulled my wagon over to the curb, dismounted and stopped a passing young man.

"Excuse me!" I asked in his language. I don't see any Jews!"

Very politely he replied, "We have no Jews!"

A little disturbed, I asked, "Where are the Jewish shopkeepers? The Jewish bookshop? The Jewish factory?

I saw the foundry was going full blast! Doesn't Yank'l still run the place?"

I could see the look of puzzlement on the man's face as I mentioned all those strange names. He took off his cap and scratched his head, trying to put together some reasonable answer.

"I remember," he said, looking into the cloudless sky, as though the answer might be there. "I remember my grandfather telling me about the time this was a small town and there were people here called, 'Jews' but I have never seen any. And the foundry was taken over by the government for military production. They have over two hundred workers around the clock! I'm sorry mister but I have to run."

I thanked him as he disappeared down the street, a street that used to be teeming with local people, merchants and buyers, business men and peasants. Now it was quiet, hardly a soul to be seen. Not even the children who used to get underfoot, playing their games were present. I decided to walk to the book shop. The new name had replaced, "The Plutka Book Shoppe." It was now "The Lenin Library". I entered, hoping to get a glass of tea but none was offered. I decided to sit at one of the tables to cool off when the lady in charge approached me.

Her Russian was impeccable. "What can I do for you, Comrade stranger?"

How did she know that I was a stranger? Was it my clothes, my beard. The skullcap under the cap that I had removed? "Nothing," I replied in Ukrainian. She understood and smiled her sympathy for an old man quite obvious. "We have a washroom in the rear, if you wish to freshen up."

I was too weary to get up, so I said, "Thank you! Could I have a moment of your time? A few questions! Please!" She remained standing, which made it difficult for me to keep looking up at her but I proceeded. "This used to be a book store! I used to come in here and enjoy a hot glass of tea."

She interrupted. "Would you like a tea? Forgive me!" She left me and returned with a glass, steaming hot. "We don't serve tea in the library but we have an old samovar in the back for the staff. What book did you have in mind?"

While she was getting the tea, my mind flipped through all those years, the names: Yushka Gonif, Yank'l the blacksmith, Feyvil Friendly, Shem Shlemazl, Gershom Gossip and so many more. Should I ask about them?" It was obviously a slow day, because she sat down and savored a tea, also.

I began by explaining that I was a book merchant and I traveled from town to town. I had become especially fond of this town, Plutka and had become friends with many of the shop keepers. But to my dismay, all of the people that I knew and loved were gone. Was I dreaming or hallucinating? She listened patiently and took pains to explain that she herself was new to Plutka, that she had been assigned by the bureau in Moscow about a year ago. Actually, she confessed, her interest in the town's history led her to read about it in the pile of newspapers that she found in the storage room. She also had found books in a strange language that opened from the wrong end.

That she couldn't help me was clear, and I found myself telling her about those missing people. She was a good listener and her laughter was refreshing and encouraging. It felt as though the clock slowed down because I went on forever. She sat there entranced as though my stories were fantastic. "Why don't you write them in a book!" she offered.

Pretty soon, the sun began to set and I apologized for keeping her from her work. It was four teas later since I had arrived and I had to water and feed my horse. With all the talk, I still had no clue about what happened to Plutka and all of the dear friends I had come to visit. I took the reins and led my horse down the street. Many people were rushing to their homes from work, some glancing in my direction, amused to see an old man pulling his horse. Where was I headed? To the Big Synagogue, of course. It was time for evening prayer. I may have been confused. The Synagogue was not where it was supposed to be. I stopped an elderly man for directions.

"Comrade!" he replied. "Haven't you heard? The German soldiers forced all the Jews into the synagogue and burned it to the ground. We stood around watching, listening to the screaming but there was nothing we could do. Some of our best neighbors perished that terrible day. The synagogue and every last Jew are gone!" I let out a shout of pain! I had struck my head just as my horse stopped in front of Yushka's house. What a terrible dream! But it was only a dream! I took some deep breaths and slapped my face to bring me back to reality.

Yushka greeted me as usual with brotherly enthusiasm. He hugged me and pulled me into the house where he had a hot bath waiting. The dream was so vivid, but I decided not to bother him with such foolishness! FOOLISHNESS!

Postscript

For weeks after that meeting, I deliberately worked late, so that I would catch the same train as when we met. I sat on the same bench but he never appeared. When I wrote the last story, it had to be "Foolishness!" for it was the very word Shalom Aleikhem spoke. Ironically, the ending was anything but foolishness. It constantly entered my mind, how much tribute he deserved, guiding me through a book called, "Aleikhem Shulem." So, one day after I finished the work, I decided to find out where he was buried, to honor him with a visit. The GPS got me to the Grand Central Parkway and the Interboro Parkway, now named for Jackie Robinson. She led me to Richmond Hill and onto a twisting, winding road into Mount Carmel Cemetery. I parked and entered the orange brick office building where a courteous young lady, whom I detected from the cross on her neck, was not Jewish, kindly gave me directions. She even told me that his gravestone was easily found in the Workman Circle plot, right on the pathway. A pearly white smile answered my gracious, "Thank you very much!" As I approached the immense gravestone I heard a shouting from the distance. "Mistah! Mistah!" An old man, in a black gabardine coat and a crushed velour hat came running toward me. My heart almost jumped out of my chest. As the man came close, I could see it wasn't the man in the subway or the one in the cameo on Sholem Aleikhem's tombstone. This man, holding a prayer book asked, "Mistah! You want I should make a 'Mawleh' (the prayer for the dead)?" Knowing Rabinowitz's position, I declined, handing the man a fiver. I took out my book, showed it to the cameo, placed a stone on the tomb as is the Jewish custom, and saying, "Aleikhem Shulem! Sholem Aleikhem! Mr. Rabinowitz!"

The End

GOM ZU OF GALITZIA

Ed Miller

"Gom Zu"

Ed Miller

I was a stranger in town and I stopped to water my nag at a trough. All of a sudden a man in tattered clothes and a scruffy beard takes my arm and begins to talk to me.

"I am a devout Jew and travel around the countryside looking for work, odds and ends, anything to make a penny." he begins.

"Forgive me," I try to interrupt, "I just stopped to water my horse. I really have no time..." I certainly wasn't planning to give him a handout and I certainly had no time for conversation. But he kept talking.

"They call me 'Gom Zu' (even this) but my real name is Mut'l (Marty). Why do they call me Gom Zu, you may ask? It is written in the Holy books and I devoutly believe in the Holy books, that everything that happens under G-d's heaven is 'Gom Zu L'Tovah!' meaning, 'even this is for the best'!"

I tried to wrest my arm free but to no avail. Before I could say, "Pardon me!" and get loose, he continued.

"Do you have a minute? I'll explain! Just last summer my house burned down. A tragedy! Well, everything except the brick oven and the cabinet with all the Holy books. A miracle! If it had been wintertime it would have been difficult but it was summer after all, when the house was unbearably hot from the oven and the sweltering weather. So, in reality it was a blessing. Until it was rebuilt we were free of the walls and a roof and so we could enjoy what little air there was.

"I can't argue with the logic!" I had to admit. It was intriguing.

"I'll give you another example!" he went on. "Last winter, our saintly Rabbi had a stroke. It impaired his speech and he became an invalid. Tragedy? No, a blessing. We in the congregation were tired of his long and to be honest, boring sermons but we didn't have the heart to fire him. His illness solved the whole problem for us. He had to retire. On a pension, of course."

"You were able to get another Rabbi?" I interjected.

"A sloti (dollar) a dozen!" he replied. Without a pause he went on. "Just last week I had no luck, no business, no money. I didn't have enough for my dear wife to buy a chicken for the Sabbath. Tragedy? Well not exactly. The Sabbath meal was, to say the least, meager but at least I didn't have to suffer with the terrible heartburn that I always got from my dear wife's chicken soup."

I was becoming intrigued with these tales and now made no attempt to leave. In fact I even encouraged him to go on with the word, "Nu ja! What else?"

"Being a stranger, I suppose you haven't heard that our Cantor had become deaf. A terrible tragedy, from an ear infection. Well, also a blessing in disguise. True, we in the congregation still have to listen to his off key singing at the Sabbath prayers but at least the Cantor, himself, doesn't have to hear it anymore."

Actually, he went on as though I were a long lost friend.

"Many years ago, I was well off. Not as rich a man of means as yourself but let us say, comfortable. I had a small business with some merchandise, trinkets. On one journey to a far city, I was robbed of my whole treasure. Everything! Even 'mazel', luck! A tragedy? Well not exactly! Along came a wagon filled with a poor and hungry family, down on their luck and they offered me a ride to the next town. Their oldest daughter, a beautiful girl with golden hair was forced to snuggle next to me. By the time we arrived at the town, as it was ordained, she was to be my treasure, my wife.

I had become so involved that I forgot all about my horse and buggy. I turned around to find that they were gone. Before I could ask "What happened?" Gom Zu explained.

"While I was talking to you, your horse and buggy took off down the street and ended up in a terrible crash. A tragedy! Your horse is dead and the buggy is in shambles. Still, you can see the blessing, can't you? Here you stand, safe and sound with me, when you could have been killed in the accident. Come home with me! Bathe yourself! My Golde will heat up some chicken soup! Gom Zu L'Tovah! Praised be the Lord!"

Where we left off, you recall, Mut'l, I mean Gom Zu and I were heading to his home. While we were walking, it occurred to me that my horse and buggy needed my attention, first. So we made a detour to check on it. The truth of the matter is that distance is often deceiving. What looked like dead was only a sprained foreleg which was being attended to by the town's animal doctor, who had been called to the scene of the runaway accident. The buggy merely had lost a wheel and was by no means destroyed. The town blacksmith was a wheelwright, a charitable man who had set about repairing the cart even before asking about the owner or who would pay for the service.

Up until now, I never revealed who I was or where I was headed. Not that I was ever asked or had the chance to say a word, thanks to Gom Zu. I am a man of means, thank the Lord and surely grateful to have found a town of righteous. In truth, I am the physician to the House of

Rothschild. I was on my way to the Royal palace when I stopped to water my horse. I decided to keep this a secret a while longer. But, let me not digress.

Golde set about to make us comfortable as soon as we kissed the Mezuzah and entered the modest hovel that Mut'l called his home. A glass of sweet hot tea was in our hands before we could sit down at the immaculate table. A pitcher with soap and water was offered and we washed the dust of the street from our hands and face. We each retired to the space between the oven and the back wall where we could remove our outer clothing and boots. A slightly worn but clean silk robe was offered me and someone's oversized slippers. Even a knitted skullcap was provided.

Gom Zu apologized, "Please forgive my poor home but as it is said in the Holy books, 'What one gains in wealth, he loses in humility!' No offense intended."

I replied, "It is also written that the gifts that the Lord gives us must not be refused but should be accepted with grace and praise to the Holy One!" As you can imagine, each of us had another quotation to offer as though it were a contest. Fortunately, Golde appeared with the tureen of steaming chicken soup, golden noodles and rich chicken fat floating on the top. The aroma made my hungry stomach growl. As she ladled out the broth, I could hardly wait to taste it, to compliment it.

During the meal we were silent as befits a respectable household. As soon as we finished, I expressed my appreciation for Golde's culinary skill. Not so, Mut'l. He sat there gripping his chest. I remembered his story and took immediate steps with a remedy. Fortunately, I had retrieved my black bag from the buggy and now was able to offer Mut'l some help. Upon downing the white powder and water, he felt better.

As soon as he was able, he began, "You see how 'Gom Zu' works. If you hadn't stopped to water your horse, we wouldn't have met. You never would have honored us at our home. And best of all, you wouldn't have been here to help my heartburn! Thank the Lord!"

He never asked, but I'm certain that he understood that I was a doctor. I felt that divulging my position and mission to the Court wasn't necessary. Before I took my leave, Golde had cleaned and brushed my travel weary clothing and boots. I asked Gom Zu to take me to see the Cantor. My examination showed that the ear condition was reversible and recommended a specialist in a nearby city. I also arranged for the Cantor to get singing lessons as part of his therapy. The old Rabbi got a position at the seminary where he could live and study in comfort. This was arranged for through the Baron's generosity, as was the help that the Cantor received. Before I left on my journey, I settled accounts with the blacksmith and the horse doctor who had graciously loaned me a horse so that I could continue on my way.

Mut'l's fortune also improved. When Golde went to wash the robe that I had worn, she found a small bag of gold coins. He was now able to restock his merchandise and his business has flourished ever since. As for Golde's chicken soup, it is rumored that the recipe was bought by someone in the Manischewitz family. I hope the heartburn was removed.

I don't know exactly how many people in the world are believers in Gom Zu but this I do know. As a result of this whole experience the number has at least increased by one. Praised be the Lord!

Although it is true that as Rothschild's doctor, I am very busy, I still try to keep in touch with Mut'l and Golde by mail. After a year or so, I made a special detour so that I could spend some time with them. Now their home was on a better street, a little more comfortable but not ostentatious. Heaven forbid there should be an evil eye.

Mut'l and I hugged each other, then we sat at the table to chat. Golde served some pastry and sweet tea, of course. He still traveled the countryside with the merchandise but now he had a store as well. Their new shop was located on the main thoroughfare, not far from the watering trough where we had first met. He immediately started with an apology.

"Please forgive us! Believe me, we are forever grateful for each and every coin and we debated whether we should return them to you. But Golde, in her wisdom said that it was a gift from above, so we thanked the Lord and gave a tithe to charity."

I assured them, "It was the right thing to do!" After all, it was I who was indebted to them for making me a believer in Gom Zu.

All of a sudden, a young child burst into the room. Gom Zu chided him, "Yossele! (Joey) Go back and kiss the Mezuzah!"

I was amazed that Mut'l had noticed the child's transgression.

He explained, "The time between the opening of the door and his entry into the room indicated that he didn't stop to do his duty. After all, at his age, he had to jump up to reach the Mezuzah with his hand."

I had to laugh at such perception. Then my curiosity got the better of me. "Please excuse me but who is this Yossele?"

Mut'l needed little prodding. "A few months ago, I was on the road with my wagon of merchandise. I came to a river and had to cross it on the ferry. The Polish man that ran it, warned me that the current was strong and that the weight of the wagon might be too much for the boat. I offered him additional fare because I had to get to the town of Blintz before the evening prayer. I assured him that we were in G-d's hands and he agreed to take me across."

"So everything went well?" I asked.

"Well, not exactly!" he replied. "Suddenly a strong gust of wind tore us from the tow line and we were swept downstream. In spite of my Gom Zu beliefs, I was terrified of the consequences as the ferry slid downstream out of control, in spite of the boatman's effort to get it to the far shore. I was very concerned but obviously, we have survived. Thank the Lord! And then the unforeseen!"

"What happened?" I pleaded, eager to hear his story.

"A little downstream, came a cry for help. It sounded like a calf or a bleating goat but it soon became clear that it was human. A high voiced human. I directed the ferry man toward the voice where we found Yossele dangling from a branch at the water's edge."

"What a wonder!" I remarked. "If not for the ferry's mishap you wouldn't have been there to save the boy!"

Gom Zu gave a big sigh. I could see how moved he was as he relived the whole experience. "Yes, isn't it amazing how wonders happen!" He took a big loud sip of his sweetened tea, then dipped a slice of dried almond cake into it and ate it before it could crumble into the glass.

"How does that explain the boy's presence here in your home?" I asked taking advantage of the moment's silence. "I know that you were never blessed with children."

"The sad part of it is, the boy is an orphan, a Yussem, no parents, no family. A tragedy! He's been wandering from town to town, hungry and alone. Nobody wanted him or could afford to shelter him. For a short while he stayed at a Polish shelter for orphans but the other boys kept taunting him, because he was Jewish, so he ran away."

"For how long has he been on his own?" I wondered.

"I believe more than two and a half years. Right, Yossele? When we drew him aboard he was exhausted and wet. If I had the time to spare, I would have cried but instead, I set out to get him dried, dressed and fed. After all, wasn't this another example of 'Gom Zu L'Tovah', even this is for the best?"

"No question about it!" I had to agree.

"The ferry was eventually landed and the wagon with the merchandise unloaded. Along side of me on the driver's seat sat my new helper, Yossele. I decided that if it was G-d's will for me to have rescued him, it was probably also His will for him to become my charge. We got to Blintz too late for the evening prayers but not too late for the special prayer that we make after one arrives safely from grave danger."

"Did you stay at the famous Inn in Blintz?" I inquired.

"Yes! After such a harrowing experience we welcomed a hot bath and good food. Of course, we had the specialty of the house, blintzes, freshly fried crepes named for the town, served with cottage cheese and sour cream. A meal fit for a king!"

I smiled as he described the food and hospitality. "I know!" I added. "The people of Blintz are world renowned for their blintzes."

"It was then that Yossele told me about himself and the sad nine years of his life. I offered him a temporary job as my assistant and he agreed. He wanted no pity, no charity.

We toured the route of my business together and by the time that we returned home, he was as good a merchant as I was."

"So he works in the store? I asked.

"Well not all the time." Gom Zu explained. "You see, I made a deal with him. First things, first. He must attend school, religious and secular. In his free time he can help in the business. Such a partnership I could agree upon."

"So the money that you found has come to some good, after all!" I added. "Yes! See how the Lord works. Never would I have imagined that meeting you and your giving the coins, would have saved a life."

"As the Holy book says, 'One good deed leads to another!' And what a joy it is for Golde and me to have a child in our house, even if the waif wasn't born to us."

At this time Yossele shyly came over to the table where the tin of the Almond-Mand'l bread stood open. I picked up the tin and handed it to him but he hesitated and looked to Mut'l for permission. Then he took a slice, broke it in half and returned half to the tin. Gom Zu asked him a question.

"Nu, Yossele! What did we learn in school today?"

The child replied, "We learned the Sh'ma."

Gom Zu and I both had tears in our eyes as the boy recited the Jewish creed that is written in the Mezuzah and in the heart of our people. I took my leave with joy and the knowledge that, as they say, 'Gom Zu L'Tovah', this too is for the good.

It was shortly after his Bar-Mitzvah, when he was on his way home from school, that the heavens opened up and Yossele nearly drowned in the freezing rain. It was December and there was a constant threat of snow but no one would have expected a torrential downpour. Well, in the spirit of Gom Zu, Yossele found refuge in the Catholic Church, the one he dreaded passing on his way home every day. The basement door was open and he entered, crouching down in a corner alcove, trying his best to keep his chattering teeth from giving him away. From his hiding place he could see nothing but he heard several heavy boots stamping off the wetness of the rain and then some mumbling.

Fortunately, his secular education in the Catholic school made him able to make out some of the conversation. He cupped his hand over his ears to hear better and this is what he was going to report to Mut'l, his adopted father, when he returned home.

The man with the deep voice asked the other, "What are we going to do about the Christmas fund?"

The one with the high voice, answered, "What do you mean, we? You stole the money, gambled it away and lost! It's only a few weeks away. What can we do?"

"We can try to get it back! You know that the Jew merchant always carries a lot of cash, especially during this time of year. We could help ourselves to his pouch one evening on his way home. Even if we have to hurt him a little. His kid hasn't been going with him, lately, so we probably wouldn't even have to hurt him at all."

At this point they moved off to a different place, so they could hardly be heard. The damp cold of Yossele's clothing made him shiver from the outside and the talk that he had just heard made him shiver from within. He was just about to make an attempt to leave, when the voices came back. They moved toward him, passed in front of him and passed out of the basement door into the street. He waited a while after the door was shut before he too left. He ran all the way home, not even noticing that the rain had let up.

What he had heard was too terrible for him to repeat coherently. Though he tried, his adoptive mother could not understand him. He would have to wait for Mut'l, Gom Zu to return home the next day. How could such vital information wait. He did his chores, ate his dinner nervously and slept a poor, fitful sleep.

The next day, Friday arrived and the time for Mut'l's return came and went. The smell of fresh baked Challah filled the house and Yossele finished polishing the Sabbath candlesticks. As the sun was setting, the sound of the wagon and the horses was heard approaching. Both Yossele and Golde stopped what they were doing and ran to the door. The horses had found their way home but without Gom Zu. Obviously something dreadful had happened. What if those two men had stopped him? The boy brought the team into the stable, unhitched them as fast as he could, gave them feed and saddled up his riding horse to begin the search. Even though he knew that he would be violating the sanctity of the Sabbath, he had to try to find his adopted father.

Yossele retraced the route that Mut'l would have taken. He stopped at each place the wagon would have stopped, then hurried on to the next, as fast as he could ride. In his mind he visualized the two men waylaying Mut'l, stealing his money and leaving him for dead. Through the tears in his eyes, he scoured the roadside in the twilight, fearing that he would find the body there. Though it was freezing weather, his body became soaked with sweat, the horses's breath rose in plumes of steam. Outside the town of Blintz, as you remember, home of the famous blintzes,

Yossele came upon a small peasant shack, alone, in the field by the side of the road. A strange feeling possessed him to make him stop there, to ask about Mut'l. All of the local people knew him, had done business with him, trusted him.

No sooner than Yossele dismounted than the door opened and the poor old peasant stood framed in the light of the room. To Yossele's frantic plea, the old man mumbled, "Yes! He is here!" Yossesle vaulted into the candle lit room to the straw pallet where Gom Zu lay, expecting the worst. The smile that greeted him was the best reward that he could get. No Corpse! No bloody face! No broken bones! "What did he find?" you may ask. As Sholem Aleikhem's Tevya would say, "Patience! Patience!"

It is true that the two assailants from the church lay in wait for him just beyond the peasant's shack. They were freezing and as time passed, their anger grew. When the wagon approached, they grabbed the horses' reins, stopped the wagon and jumped aboard, ready to dispatch Mut'l and grab the money. But neither the merchant nor the money was there. Angry and disappointed they left the horses to continue their way home. Mut'l, on the other hand was in the old peasant's shack, burning with a fever from a bad attack of appendicitis. The old peasant had helped him to the bed, prepared an herb tea and applied a poultice to his abdomen to relieve the pain. Mut'l obviously could not be moved. He had the horses sent on to the house where he figured that Golde and Yossele would be waiting and would understand that something had happened to him.

Yossele wanted to stay but Mut'l ordered him to rush home to inform Golde that he would be all right. This Sabbath would have to pass without him. As soon as the Havdallah prayer was made, Yossele dispatched a messenger to the Rothchild's for me to come. I did not wait for my carriage to be readied, but mounted my fastest horse, medicine bag in hand and flew to the aid of my dear friend.

The update is that, the peasant's remedy worked wonders and surgery was not necessary. After a week of care, Mut'l was able to return home where Yossele reported on what he had overheard in the church. As to the plot, the two men, being superstitious, saw the empty wagon as a sign from heaven and they subsequently confessed their theft of the church funds and plan to rob the Jew, to the priest. He advised them to do penance and admit their folly to the authorities. The old peasant, a devout Christian, refused any compensation for his act of mercy. Mut'l made a pledge to stop by the shack at least once a week to deliver food and to see that the old man's needs were always taken care of.

It is in the Jewish tradition, that when a great tragedy is averted, a feast is held, called "Purim Sheinie".(second

Purim) As we sat around the table to celebrate Mut'l's recovery, he gave a prayer of thanks. "The terrible rainstorm was bad but then Yossele wouldn't have overherad the vile plot. The appendicitis attack was terribly dangerous but if not for that, I might have gone on to be robbed and killed by the two men. If not for the old peasant, I might have died from the appendicitis, leaving my dear wife a widow and Yossele, my son, orphaned twice. What mysteries we behold!" As he raised his eyes to heaven, he continued. "And all of these misfortunes, how grave they might be, all have turned out for the best. Gom Zu L'tovah!"

By the time the Festival of Chanukah arrived, Mut'l was well enough to join his family in front of the Menorah. As the flames burned the olive oil, a warm glow enveloped them all. Their songs of praise celebrating the miracle of the Temple had a special meaning. Soon Golde's latkes-potato pancakes would sizzle on the fire but Mut'l could not enjoy them this time. Doctor's orders. Golde wept silent tears of thanks for her own miracle. Her husband had been saved.

All along the way, Gom Zu found examples of this motto. And with each tragedy, his fortunes increased. It was like a charm and it seemed as though Mut'l actually sought adversity to reap the benefits. He became wealthy, now seldom leaving the store to take to the road. Yossele had grown into a fine young man and was sought after by the high and the mighty. He and one of Rothchild's beautiful daughters were to be married and the royal court was buzzing with the thought of a magnificent wedding. Mut'l's station in life became so high that he held a seat of honor on the Eastern wall of the synagogue. He had become Mordechai, the noble, the G'vir. He wore fine gabardine suits, shaved his beard and flaunted his success shamelessly. He dressed his Golde in the finest silks. Decorated her with gold and diamonds. Her culinary talent of which you have heard before, also blossomed. As I said before, I cannot absolutely affirm it, but I suspect a special horse-radish recipe, named for her, has become popular all over the world, especially at Passover time.

But this is a digression. Gom Zu had become opportunistic, avaricious and selfish. His acts of charity were calculated and he forgot his humble beginnings. He became more interested in his weekly balance than his employees or his patrons. Yearly his vest size increased as did his bank account. Every so often, he would visit the House of the Rothchilds and I would warn him that his heart could not take the strain of his corpulence. He would merely laugh, puff on his Turkish cigar and say, "Gom Zu L'tovah!" Look how my tailor gets rich and my man-servant lives off of tying my shoes? I grieved to see what had become of that simple soul whom I met at the watering trough so long ago.

At my insistence, he made a will which took care of all the important matters of a future without him. To his credit, he did remember those who had helped twist fate in his favor. But he never lived to see his beloved Yossele under the chupah, wedding canopy. Soon after the nuptials were arranged, the expected happened and this time there was nothing to change fate, not even for Gom Zu. A special coffin had to be built of cedar. A gold embroidered tallis was placed around his shoulders and the white kittle-shroud in which he was buried. Hundreds attended his funeral. Few mourned him. Josef's (Yossele) grief was apparent as he recited the Kaddish-mourner's prayer. Golde fainted as the body was lowered into the grave. There were many eulogies, for his money had bought him great honor. This was the end for my friend, Mut'l, Gom Zu.

I joined the family in the Shiva-days of mourning. One night, I had a fitful sleep. I had a dream. There was Mut'l, as big as life, standing before the heavenly court. He was no Buncha Shveig. When his record was read by the Archangel Michael, he constantly interrupted with extenuating circumstances. He appealed to the court's compassion but it was rebuffed. Even the overriding philosophy, Gom Zu L'tovah, was thrown in his face. After all, what had he done with all of the chances he was given? What! It took no time at all for his heavenly rest to be denied. My shout of disappointment woke me up. I was so upset that I found it hard to fall back to sleep again. After some time, I nodded off.

This time in my dream, I found Mut'l seated at the head of a long table, dimly lit by a small candle, about to go out. Strangely, it never actually died. Seated all around him at the table were all the dead souls of evil and vile men, who had forsaken G-d and man in their lives. In front of Mut'l were all the sacred texts that were spared when his house had burned down, as you recall. Now he was condemned to teach the damned from the holy books, a look of complete confusion on their faces. Mut'l, however, had a happy smile on his face, his eyes sparkled with unimaginable joy. "You see, my friends," he seemed to be addressing the congregation of the dead and me as well. "What would I be doing in heaven with all the righteous, learned, wise and G-d-fearing souls? Here, at least I have a mission, to teach G-d's words. What greater reward is there for a soul like mine. As it is written in the Holy books, "To everything there is a reason or is it season...?" See! As I've always believed, Gom Zu L'tovah! Even this is for the best! Baruch Ha'shem! Blessed be His Name!"

*   *   *

The End

Edwards Brothers Malloy
Oxnard, CA USA
January 14, 2016